CHALKBOARD PREACHER

FROM VINEGAR BEND

Book I
Vinegar Bend Series

KAY CHANDLER

A MULTI-AWARD-WINNING AUTHOR

This novel is a work of fiction. Names, characters, places and incidents are products of the author's imagination or used fictitiously.

Scripture taken from the King James Version of the Holy Bible

Cover Design by Chase Chandler

DEDICATED TO A PREACHER'S WIFE

I'd like to dedicate this book to my sweet friend, **Beverly Shirah**, one of the Godliest women I know. Though she's endured countless hardships on this earth, including losing a beloved son, her faith in the Lord Jesus Christ has never wavered.

This one's for you, Bev!

Note from the Author:

In the early 1900's, my maternal great-grandfather, John Henry Redd, Sr., carried his young son, Will, to a schoolhouse to hear Dr. Charles Lofton lecture as he illustrated his sermon in startling sketches on the blackboard. While there, John Henry purchased Dr. Lofton's book of chalkboard drawings, copyright 1898. The book was passed down to me and is now in possession of my grandson, Samuel Chandler. The peculiar chalk drawings have always fascinated me, and I have chosen to share a few of them in my novel.

My paternal great-grandfather was Reverend Charlie McDurmont, a noted circuit-rider preacher who lived during the same era. Charlie's wife, Fendora died, leaving ten children behind. My grandmother, Sallie was a baby at the time. Charlie then married sixteen-year-old Rebekah, and together they had six more children. When Charlie was notified his beloved Rebekah had succumbed, he fell dead upon hearing the news. It was said he died of a broken heart, and they were buried together.

These men were my inspiration for writing Chalkboard Preacher from Vinegar Bend. I hope you enjoy.

PROLOGUE

July 19, 1917

Dear Rebekah,

I received your letter Friday last, and have prayed diligently, seeking Godly counsel concerning your desire to come live with me. Now, having received my answer, it is with a heart filled with deep trepidation that I must decline your humble request.

My dear, it breaks my heart to pen this letter for I fear you won't understand. Yet, for both our sakes, I simply cannot permit it. I'm an old woman and have lived alone with my six precious cats far too long to share my house with anyone at this point in my life.

I am afraid my brother has a bit of the devil himself in him, but how any man could be so cruel to his own flesh and blood is beyond my comprehension. If your mother was alive, she wouldn't allow Lonnie to treat you in such a wicked way, but I think he snapped when Lois died giving birth. I've always felt he blames you for her death and after receiving your heart-wrenching letter, describing his cruel attitude toward you, I am convinced I was right.

I waited until now to answer your letter, because I wanted to talk to the Reverend Castle Marlowe—or Brother Cass, as he is affectionately known—before getting your hopes up. Whether the forthcoming thought was from God or from my own desire to free you from a troublesome situation, I cannot say. However, please hear me out. If it is of God it will surely stand, but if not, it will quickly come to naught.

Brother Cass is a Chalkboard Preacher from Vinegar Bend who travels the circuit, illustrating his sermons on the blackboard in rural schoolhouses. Such a talented artist, I dare say the frightening sketches would make even the sorriest sinner repent. Although I sometimes have trouble sleeping at night after his lectures, I've learned a lot about what it means to draw nigh to God and resist the devil.

He lost his wife nigh a year ago, leaving a newborn behind. So sad, it was. All young'uns need a mama, but who would know that better than you? To add to his troubles, the baby's nanny died back in May. I don't know how the poor man has managed to find time to prepare his wonderful lectures, keep up his responsibilities at home, and travel with so many depending upon him.

Here's the good news. As God would have it, Brother Cass was due to lecture here in State Line last Sunday, so I invited him home with me and prepared a lavish Sunday dinner. The way he downed that fried chicken and banana pudding, one would've thought he hadn't eaten in months.

After dinner, I informed him I had a niece who was considering a move, and would he be interested in having you come live with him to cook and manage his household. I had no idea if he'd be receptive to the idea, but I watched as he pushed away from the table, rubbed his chin and stared out the window. It was plain to see from the pain on his face that he had come to his wit's end. He asked several questions, such as if you had children, if you'd ever been married, and if you were a God-fearing woman. I answered as best I could, but I saw no need to tell him you were in such dire straits, nor did I mention that I haven't seen you since you were three or four years old.

Being a man of deep thought, he was slow to respond. Then, after what seemed an eternity, he leaned in and with his elbows planted on the table, he said. "I'll do it." Just like that, he said it. "I'll do it." He gave me money to send to you for a train ticket, which I have enclosed. He said tell you to meet him at the train station in Vinegar Bend, July 22. I was in a state of shock when he added, "Tell her my friend, Judge Rex Roy will marry us as soon as she arrives." You could've knocked me over with a feather, yet I never cease to be amazed at the wondrous works of God. Of course, I should've known he couldn't afford to set himself up for idle gossip by having a woman living in the same household; yet, marriage is exceedingly abundant more than you and I could have ever asked or hoped for.

Lois was only fifteen when she and my brother married, and Lonnie was eighteen with a headful of high hopes. I'll never forget how happy they were when they learned she was in the family way. Two people have never been so in love. What a pity that joy was soon turned to mourning.

Dear, I'm sure you'll be as beautiful a bride as your sweet mother. Brother Cass is a very gentle man and he'll be good to you. God has answered our prayers, Rebekah. I know you'll be a blessing to one another.

Love,

Aunt Nellie

P.S. You might wish to pack a lunch to eat on the train. It'll be a long train ride from Sipsey Ridge to Vinegar Bend.

CHAPTER 1

Rebekah McAlister sat cross-legged in the loft—not so close to the opening that her papa could see her if he should come home early and catch her reading, but close enough to enjoy a breeze if the Good Lord should choose to send a refreshing breath of air her way.

She unbuttoned the straps to her overalls and let the bib fall to her waist. Then pulling her long dark braids up and securing them with a comb on top of her head, she wiped sweat from her neck with the tail of her shirt. According to the rusty thermometer nailed on the side of the barn, the temperature had soared to a scorching ninety-four degrees, and the Alabama high humidity made it almost impossible to breathe. From her vantage point, she could see over the top of the two-room log cabin she shared with her Papa. Now, that she thought about it, she supposed it was the only thing they'd ever shared. She gazed at the field on the other side of the dirt road at the dying corn stalks, signaling the beginning of the end of a long, hot summer.

A book by Louisa May Alcott lay closed on her lap. Rebekah was a voracious reader and books had always been her way of escaping reality. The first book she remembered reading was Cinderella. As a child, she entertained foolish thoughts of meeting her own handsome Prince who would sweep her away on the back of his white horse, take her to live in a castle and buy her a pair of shoes and beautiful dresses.

But she was no longer a child. She was sixteen years old and experienced enough to know that dreams never come true and true nightmares never end. Yet, such bitter knowledge had never prevented her from longing for a better way of life. If only she could be like Jo, her favorite character in Little Women and have three sisters and a special friend—a friend such as Laurie—she could tolerate anything. But she had no one. No one except Papa.

After opening her book to the dog-eared page where she left off, she read the same chapter over for the third time before slamming it shut. Her mind wasn't on the adventures of Jo and Laurie, but on a dreadful letter tucked inside the pocket of her overalls. Laying the book aside, she stretched out on the hay.

For days, she'd waited in eager anticipation for her aunt's reply, and for Aunt Nellie to respond with such a ridiculous suggestion was almost insulting. Rebekah could understand why an old maid might not wish to share her home, but the preposterous implication that God would have her marry a stranger and raise someone else's baby came nowhere close to a rational solution.

Marriage hadn't worked out so well for her mama and papa and according to her aunt, they were madly in love. Rebekah was desperate but not insane. Nevertheless, Aunt Nellie meant well and deserved a reply. Turning the letter over, she pulled a pencil from behind her ear and wrote on the back of the paper, since her father had refused to give her money to buy a writing tablet.

Dear Aunt Nellie,

I appreciate the lengths you have gone to in order to help me, and no doubt the preacher is a fine man and would treat me kindly. However, . . . She stopped, clamped the pencil between her teeth and skimmed over the letter searching for a date. "July 22?"

There was no way her response could reach State Line in two days. With a sigh, Rebekah once again put the pencil to the paper and picked up where she left off. *However, since it is now the twentieth of the month, I regret this letter will not reach you in time to notify the preacher that I won't be at the train station. I apologize for any inconvenience I may have caused either of you. You were kind to want to help, Aunt Nellie. Please inform the preacher I will be praying for the Lord to send him a helpmate, but it shall not be me.*
Your loving niece,
Rebekah

Aunt Nellie was her last hope. She'd still be under the tyrant's roof until the day one of them died and from all appearances, Lonnie McAlister was in excellent health. Rebekah sometimes wished her papa would go ahead and strike her with that horrid strap so she could stop dreading it. Though he'd never struck her with it, the act couldn't be worse than the constant fear.

The peaceful silence was suddenly interrupted by an all too familiar clopping sound in the distance. Turning over on the hay, she saw her father's wagon coming down the dusty, dirt road, much earlier than expected. She quickly buckled the strap to her overalls and in her haste to get away from the barn, her foot slipped on a broken rung on the rickety ladder, causing her to fall to the hard ground. Though her elbow smarted, she jumped up, ran through the back door, darted into the house, and managed to be on the front stoops before her father stepped from the wagon.

"You're home earlier than usual, Papa. I suppose it's a good sign."

His face reddened when he growled. "A good sign? You beat all girl, the way you talk in riddles. What's good about it?"

"I simply meant you must've sold all the vegetables, or you wouldn't be home so early."

"I didn't sell diddly squat. Bert Haskell drove around on his new truck and beat me to every house in the County. After hearing the same spiel from every customer, that his vegetables are fresher than mine, I quit and came home. Liars. Every last one of 'em. Ain't no way his vegetables are fresher."

"Then why do you suppose they would prefer to buy from Mr. Haskell, Papa?"

"That's a stupid question. If I knew, don't you think I'd turn the tables on him?" His voice roared. "They want fresh? I'll give 'em fresh. Make yourself useful, girl. Throw the vegetables that are in the back of the wagon to the hogs and water the mule." With that, he stormed off toward the house.

Rebekah fed the hogs, unbridled the mule, then led him to the barn. She was putting up the wagon when Lonnie opened the screen door and hollered. "Would somebody please tell me why my supper ain't on the stove? I'll tell you why. You've been lying around reading them books of yours all day. That's why."

Peculiar how Papa always called on "somebody" when there were only the two of them living there and then demanded explanations for what he already knew.

He yelled, "I oughta burn every last one of them books," then slammed the door.

It wasn't the first time he'd threatened to burn her books. Perhaps one day he'd make good on his many threats. Her books were a gift from her former schoolteacher, and Rebekah had read all five of them countless times, yet never tired of reliving the exciting adventures.

After attending her chores, Rebekah trudged into the house. "I wasn't expecting you for several more hours, Papa, or I would've started supper before now. It won't take me long." She gnawed on her fist, as she watched him unbuckle his belt.

"You won't never learn, will you, girl? I'm gonna teach you one of these days that I say what I mean, and I mean what I say." He doubled the strap in his hand, then ambled over across the room and hung it on a nail by the back door. Rebekah blew out a soft breath, then watched as he picked up a fly swatter and swung at a horse fly.

His voice boomed. "What are you looking at?"

"Nothing, Papa." She reached up and pulled the comb from her hair, allowing her braids to fall.

"Well, if you don't hurry and get viddles on the table, I'll give you something to look at." His icy glare sent chills inching up her spine.

"Go get me the scissors."

"Scissors, Papa?"

"You heard me."

She walked over and picked up the sewing basket from off the mantle, pulled out the scissors and handed to her father.

Grabbing her arm with a firm hand, he tightened his grip.

"You're hurting me, Papa. What are you doing?" She clamped her hand over her mouth when he lifted the scissors toward her head. In one swift clip, a braid fell to the floor. She stood rigid as he tugged at the hair on the opposite side of her head. The other braid landed on her shoulder before hitting the floor.

Handing the scissors to her, he stalked back over to his chair and proceeded to pull off his boots.

Her voice quivered as her hand reached up to touch her hair. "Why, Papa?"

"If you'd spent as much time in the kitchen as you did braiding your hair, I'd be eating by now."

Rebekah rolled out a baker of biscuits and placed a large slice of ham in the iron skillet. Tears streamed down her face as the ham popped and sizzled, but her mind was no longer on her father's dreaded strap. *He hates me. Even Aunt Nellie said as much.* Her thoughts were focused on the words Aunt Nellie wrote when quoting the preacher: "*Just like that, he said, 'I'll do it'*" Catching her bottom lip between her teeth, she whispered, "Well, I'll do it, too, by Jiminy."

After supper, her papa grabbed a croaker sack and headed for the field. When she followed him out the door, he turned and scowled. "Where do you think you're going?"

"To help you gather the vegetables?"

"There ain't that much left in the fields and besides, I'd rather do it myself than put up with your senseless chatter."

Sensing from his tone, she surmised he felt guilty for snipping off her hair, but he had no need to fret about her talking too much. Rebekah had absolutely nothing more to say to him. She was done.

After washing the two plates and wiping down the iron skillet, she pulled Aunt Nellie's letter from her pocket, glanced over her response on the back, then tore it up. The lump in her throat swelled as she ran her fingers through her short hair. Trudging to her room, she went to bed early.

At the sound of her papa's footsteps on the porch, Rebekah clinched her eyes shut, pretending to be asleep.

CHAPTER 2

July 22, 1917

After a restless night of tossing and turning, Rebekah arose at three-thirty a.m. to prepare her father's breakfast. She had an unfamiliar queasy feeling in her stomach. Granted, the thought of marrying a stranger would be a valid reason to be fearful, but Rebekah was confident the peculiar feeling wasn't fear related. She knew those feelings of scorpions in the gut, all too well. No, this was more like butterflies flitting around inside her. Was it possible this was what hope felt like?

She reached up and stroked her bobbed hair. What if he took one look at her and turned her away? If only she'd left a day earlier. With a shrug she attempted to convince herself it wouldn't matter to a desperate preacher what she looked like. Judging from the questions he asked Aunt Nellie, it was evident the man was only interested in a wife who could tend to a baby and take care of the household duties. There had been no mention of her appearance.

After breakfast, Rebekah watched out the window and by the light of a full moon saw her papa lift himself on to the wagon and ride out of the yard.

Her carpetbag was packed and under her bed. When the wagon pulled onto the road, she ran outside, took a shower, and washed her hair in the make-shift shower near the well, which she was forbidden to use. He'd say, "There's a pump in the kitchen and a tub on the porch," when she'd ask permission to shower. After scrubbing her hair until the strands squeaked like a noisy wheel, she dried off, then ran into the house. She headed straight for Papa's room, opened the trunk, pulled out a pink gingham-checked dress and prayed it would fit. Rebekah recalled the day she saw Papa sitting on the side of his bed, holding that dress with tears rolling down his cheeks. When she asked about it, he jumped up and slammed the door without answering, but she knew. She knew by the way he held it tightly and rubbed it across his face that it was indeed her mother's. And she knew by the tears that her papa loved her mama. If only he could've loved her, too. For years, she'd longed to examine the contents in the trunk but there was no time to plunder, since she had a train to catch. She ran her fingers over a beautiful three-piece boxed dresser set with a silver brush, comb and mirror that lay on top, then picked up a lovely wide-brimmed picture hat and placed it on her head.. Slamming the trunk shut, her heart raced. She wanted to believe she wasn't stealing. Weren't her mother's things as much hers as they were Papa's? Her rightful inheritance? But Papa would be furious when he discovered she'd taken the items from the trunk. This arrangement with the preacher had to work. There was no turning back, now.

The dress was a mite wrinkled but the fit couldn't have been more perfect. Whirling around in front of the mirror, the full skirt spread out into a circular motion, reminding her of a morning glory popping open in the early morn. She placed her hands on her tiny waist and glared at the way the darts in the bodice accented the figure she never knew she had. Even with wet, short hair Rebekah felt more beautiful than she'd ever felt in her life. It was the first time she'd ever worn anything other than boys' baggy overalls. She tried not to focus on her hair, which reached her waist before her papa got hold of the scissors. At least it wasn't as short as it could've been. It almost touched her shoulders. Almost.

She twirled the hat around on her finger, admiring its beauty. It was the loveliest hat she'd ever seen. Yellow straw covered with netting and a big pink ribbon the same shade as the gingham dress. Then, looking down at her feet, she groaned.

Perhaps the preacher wouldn't care about her hair, but didn't she hear somewhere that it was a sin for a woman to let a man see her bare feet? Rebekah didn't know much about such things, but it was one more thing to worry about. What if the preacher changed his mind about marrying her when he saw her naked feet? What if? Where would she go? There'd be no way she could ever go home again. Attempting to dismiss the frightening thoughts, she scribbled on the top of the salt box, "Bye, Papa." She supposed she owed him that much.

Rebekah's throat tightened as she raked through her long wet hair with her mother's wide, flat brush. Hurriedly checking the contents of her bag, she double-checked to make sure she hadn't forgotten anything: both muslin shirts, her overalls and the two pair of step-ins she made from a flour sack. Grabbing her nightgown she rolled it tightly, then packed it, along with her mother's silver dresser set.

She was making the right decision for everyone concerned. Wasn't she? Wasn't everyone getting what they really wanted? Even though he'd be furious that she took the dress, hat and dresser set, Papa would be relieved she was gone since she'd been a thorn in his flesh from the day she was born. A preacher wouldn't be expecting a wife in the real sense of the word. All he needed was someone to cook, clean and tend to the baby and she could do that for him. But what did she want? After pondering the question, she whispered, "To be thought worthy." That was it. All her life, Rebekah had longed for acceptance.

Gazing one last time at her image in the mirror, she wondered if he'd look her over, glance down at her dusty feet and dismiss her as nothing more than a dirty, barefoot waif?

When a sudden thought flashed through her mind, she ran to the kitchen and pulled a clean wash rag from the cupboard drawer and tucked it in her skirt pocket. Then pumping water into a pint jar, she screwed the top on tight and stuck it in the carpetbag. She might not have shoes, but she'd make sure her feet were clean before meeting her intended.

There was a slight breeze in the air, enough to dry her wet hair as she trudged down the dusty road to town. By the time Rebekah reached the depot her hair had dried in ringlets. She placed the hat on her head and tied the ribbon under her chin.

The train ride was even more exciting than she had imagined. The nagging doubts had subsided, and she was glad she finally garnered the courage to leave. Papa had long made it known she was a nuisance and would be happy to have her out of the house. He constantly complained about her cooking and said she talked too much.

Rebekah wanted to believe the preacher was a desperate man and the fact she had no shoes and her bobbed hair barely touched her collar would be of little importance to him. Though she knew nothing about the man she was about to marry, Aunt Nellie assured her he was a gentle man and gentle sounded good. Real good. Even the thought of caring for his baby as if it were her own, no longer frightened her. She'd be the kind of stepmother she wished her papa had married. If the baby was a girl, she'd read Cinderella to her as soon as she could understand. The spontaneous notion brought a smile to her lips. Maybe the baby was a boy and would like to hear about Robin Hood.

A rather sophisticated looking lady sat across the aisle.

Judging from the lines between the woman's eyes and the downward-turned mouth, it was evident she was either extremely sad or very lonely and no one was more familiar with those feelings than Rebekah. Feeling she'd explode if she didn't make an effort to initiate a conversation, yet recalling her papa's complaint that she talked too much, she resisted as long as she could. The moment she caught the woman glance her way, she smiled and thrust out her hand.

"Hello. My name's Rebekah and I'm on my way to a place in South Alabama called Vinegar Bend."

The woman made an incoherent mumble and turned her head to look out the window.

"That's a mighty pretty broach you're wearing, ma'am. Is that a real ruby?"

She jerked around and glared at Rebekah. "It is indeed."

Proud of the progress she was making, Rebekah said, "Where may I ask are you going?"

The lines between the woman's eyes deepened into two deep trenches. Without answering the question, she asked one of her own. "A chorus girl?"

Rebekah discreetly turned her head to look behind her, then with her hand cupped over her mouth, she whispered, "Where?"

What happened next was not Rebekah's imagination. It was an eyeroll. The woman definitely rolled her eyes.

"I pride myself on being able to guess a person's line of work. Take the man sitting on the second seat. He's a lawyer."

Rebekah was more interested in seeing the chorus girl but craned her neck to get a better look at the bald, pudgy man up front. "Not that I'm disputing you, but how do you know?"

"I make it a habit to spend my time observing more and talking less and I'm seldom wrong about people. I'd say you're going to Vinegar Bend to work in a saloon. Am I right?"

Puzzled why anyone would mistake her for a chorus girl, she wanted to believe it was meant to be a compliment and took it as such. "Well, I do declare. That's amazing. Folks say I sing like a bird, yet you've never heard me sing. I reckon you guessed right away that I have a singing voice, just from hearing me talk."

Her lip curled upward in a snarl. "I have no idea if you can sing. But it's my understanding that chorus girls don't have to carry a tune if they're pretty to look at and can prance around on a stage. Your bobbed hair was a giveaway. I sized you up as soon as you sat down." She glanced down at Rebekah's feet and abruptly shifted her position to glare out the window.

Rebekah quickly pulled her legs under the seat. If the woman was lonely or sad, it was her own fault. She was meaner than a rattlesnake. The surge of confidence that had lifted Rebekah's spirits when she saw herself all dolled up in her mother's dress and hat, quickly seeped out, the way air seeps out of a balloon when pricked with a pin. Would the preacher have the same reaction as the snooty woman? Not ever having seen a real chorus girl, perhaps the woman was right. Maybe she did fit the description. What would she do if he took one look and changed his mind?

When the woman appeared to be asleep, Rebekah reached in her pocket for the dry rag and attempted to wipe her feet and legs as best she could, though the dirt around her toenails was there to stay.

The smell of fried chicken coming from the seat behind her made her wish she'd taken Aunt Nellie's advice to pack a lunch. A sausage biscuit left over from breakfast would have satisfied the craving in her stomach.

Attempting to focus on something other than hunger pains, she shifted her thoughts to the changes about to take place in her life. What would she call her new husband? Brother Cass? Reverend Cass? Preacher? Was he tall, short, fat, thin, bald or a headful of unruly hair? One thing she could count on—he'd be homely to look at. Weren't most preachers? At least the only three she'd ever known were. If he was comely to look at, he would've had no trouble finding a wife from within his congregation which included six different communities. Suited her fine that no other woman wanted him.

She shivered as she recalled her papa's wide leather strap and the constant threats that kept her awake at night.

Rebekah cherished the idea of going to bed at night and getting a good night's sleep. She knew preachers didn't make much money, and she was okay with that. Anything would be more than what she was accustomed to, but she did hope he had a nice plump feather mattress for her bed and not a straw-filled one like the one she had back home. The straw was forever finding a way to poke through the ticking and stick in her.

Her bottom lip suddenly caught between her teeth as a sick feeling swept over her. What was she thinking? This wasn't some fairytale she was living out. She was about to become a married woman.

Sweat popped out on her brow as she attempted to dispel a frightening thought that she hadn't taken time to consider until now. As his wife, would he expect her to—no. Of course, not. He was a preacher, for goodness sake. Her stomach knotted. *So, he's a preacher. A preacher who had a wife . . . who had a baby. His baby.* Her throat was so dry she couldn't swallow. She pulled out the pint jar and drank the water with which she packed to wash her feet.

CHAPTER 3

"Next stop, Vinegar Bend," the conductor shouted as the train slowed.

With her palm, Rebekah wiped dust from the window and gazed out, diligently searching for her intended. The locomotive jolted and the conductor rose from his seat and strolled down the aisle. "I believe this is where you get off, little lady."

"Yes, thank you." She reached under her seat and grabbed her carpet bag. Stepping off, she spotted a young fellow leaning against a post at the depot, chewing on a broom straw. He appeared to scrutinize each passenger as they disembarked, though there were only three of them.

Since he was the only one who seemed to be expecting someone, Rebekah held her head high, straightened her back and strode toward him. Feigning confidence, she grasped her carpet bag with both hands, and announced, "I'm Rebekah."

He chewed on what appeared to be a broom straw and looked her over from her bobbed hair to her bare feet. "Yeah?"

She glanced away. Her lip trembled. Why was he making this so hard for her? Was he changing his mind? She turned abruptly when a smartly dressed gentleman, thirty years or about, walked over, took off a fine-looking Stetson hat and held it against his chest. Judging from the troubled look on his face, she assumed something dreadful had recently happened to him.

Fumbling with his hat, he stammered. "Excuse me, but. . . did either of you happen to see a woman, uh, perhaps about my age, step off the train?"

Rebekah said, "No, sir. There were only three of us who got off here—just me and an elderly couple. Sorry." As usual, her imagination ran wild and she presumed his wife was supposed to be on the train. Maybe she ran off with another fellow. But that wouldn't make sense. He wasn't bad-looking and he had such a nice, gentle voice. Feeling the need to comfort, she said, "Maybe your wife missed the train and will be on the afternoon run." She shrugged. "But you didn't say she was your wife, did you?"

Her words didn't appear to sink in. He scratched his head. "I don't understand. Are you sure there was no one else?"

"Very sure."

The young man took the straw from his mouth. "She's right, Preacher. I was standing here when it pulled up."

Rebekah's brow raised. "Preacher? You're a preacher?"

"You say that it as if it's a bad thing, miss."

"I'm sorry. It caught me by surprise. My name is Rebekah. Does that mean anything to you?"

His tanned face turned blood red. "You? You can't be. You're so young."

Her teeth ground together. "Well, I'm as shocked as you are. You're so . . . so . . . "

He grinned. "So old?" He let out a heavy breath. "Maybe we should sit out here on the bench and discuss the situation. You are not what I was expecting."

"You were hoping for someone prettier, weren't you? I know I'm skinny."

"Not skinny at all. You're very beautiful." The way he blushed, he appeared to be embarrassed by his own words. "You're just so young."

She shrugged. "Well, I may be young, but I've tended babies before. I kept Miz Annie's baby for over three months when she had TB and had to go to the sanitorium, so if you're still willing to marry me, I reckon I'm willing to go through with it."

He sat beside her, leaned over and put his face in his hands. "You seem like a good kid, I think we were both misled. I'm sure you pictured me as someone nearer your age. Why don't I go inside and buy you a ticket and send you back home?"

Rebekah could hold back the tears no longer. "No. I can't," she sobbed. "I can see you're disappointed. You don't have to marry me if you don't want to, but I can't go back. I just can't. Papa will be furious. I'll die if I have to go back."

He glanced at his watch. "No need for tears. Let's think. What about your Aunt Nellie? I can take you to her house."

She shook her head vigorously. "I pleaded with her to let me live with her, but she gave me a dozen excuses. I ain't going where I ain't wanted. I'll get a job in a saloon first. If you think I'm pretty, maybe they will, too. I've been told that's the only requirement to work there."

His eyes squinted into tiny slits. "Rebekah, are you saying you'd marry me, even though I'm old enough to be your father?"

"Yessir. I will. I'll marry you and I'll try hard to do anything you ask me to do." She sucked in a lungful of air. "Anything."

"How old are you, anyway?"

She lowered her head. "I'd planned to lie to you and tell you I was eighteen, but I'm afraid the Lord might strike me dead for lying to one of his messengers. Truth is, I'm going on seventeen."

He ran his hands through his hair and clinched his eyes shut. She waited for him to speak.

"Good gravy. So you're only sixteen. You could've fooled me. I knew you were young, but I could've easily believed you to be eighteen. Even nineteen. But *sixteen*?"

She shrugged. "I'll admit, I expected you to be much younger, but makes no difference to me. Besides, I'll be seventeen soon. Plenty of girls my age are married with two or three young'uns already. Look, all I need is a place to stay and you need someone to keep house, cook and of course, tend to the baby."

From the faraway look on his tanned, weathered face, she wasn't sure he'd heard a word she said. Without making eye contact, he reached down by the bench and grabbed her carpetbag.

"We'd better hurry. The judge from Chatom is a friend of mine, and he's attending a convention at the hotel this week."

Not a word was spoken by either of them as Brother Cass drove a few blocks and parked in front of the largest brick hotel she'd ever seen.

Rebekah's eyes darted from one side of the enormous lobby to the other. The chubby cherubs painted on the ceiling made her smile, and the gorgeous chandelier must've had two-hundred prisms, casting diamond-like reflections. The preacher led her down a wide corridor with doors on either side until they reached an elevator. Rebekah had never ridden an elevator and would've preferred using the stairs, but she wasn't given a choice. It slowly rose, then stopped with a loud thud, causing her to lose her balance and fall into the arms of the preacher. She quickly regained her balance and wondered if her face was as red as his.

They stopped in front of a door with the number 412. Before the preacher had an opportunity to knock, the door opened and a distinguished looking man, looking all wide-eyed, stepped out and slapped Cass across the back. "Blow me down, if it's not my ol' buddy, Cass! What a surprise. If you'd been two minutes later, you would've missed me. I was just about to go down to the restaurant for dinner. I'd be pleased if you and your daughter would join me." He patted Rebekah on the head. "You sure have grown. I wouldn't have recognized you, sugar."

The preacher took off his hat and crumpled it in his hands. "Rex, I want you to marry me."

The man chuckled. "Sorry, friend, but I'm already taken. Besides, Edna is better looking than you. Seriously, what can I do for you?"

The preacher pulled at the neck of his shirt, as if he were choking. "It's no joke. I read in the paper last week that you'd be here, and I arranged my schedule in order to have you marry me." He stepped aside and gave a toss of his head in Rebekah's direction. "To her."

The judge made no attempt to hide his shock. "No wonder I didn't recognize her. I assumed she was your daughter. Uh . . . so how long have you two been courting?"

"We haven't courted. I just met her today."

His bushy brows met in the middle. "I see." He stroked his chin. "No, I take that back. I don't see. Come on in and let's talk about this before you make such a momentous decision."

"The decision is made already. We just need you to marry us."

The judge's eyes darted from her face to her feet. If he tried to hide his shock, he did a poor job. His jovial tone turned somber. "Miss, have a seat. I'd like to talk with you both privately. This is a huge step and I would be derelict of my duties if I didn't take time to counsel you both before uniting you in holy matrimony. Cass, I'd like to question you first, so step with me into the other room."

The judge opened a door to an adjoining room, stepped aside and waited for the preacher to enter. Before closing the door, he turned to Rebekah and sounding quite condescending, said, "Miss, please excuse us. This shouldn't take long. There's a new Life

Magazine on the desk, if you'd like to browse through it while you wait. You'll find it has a lot of interesting pictures to look at."

Rebekah bristled at the insinuation she might not know how to read.

The door closed and the two men stood eye-to-eye. Their gaze locked. The judge spoke first. "I can see you're sweating."

"Then you won't mind if I shed this coat. It was a hot ride." He hung the coat on the back of a chair. "Rex, it'll soon be dark, and I need to get this over with, so whatever you have to say, I'd be obliged if you wouldn't beat around the bush."

"Man, what in tarnation are you thinking? Have you lost your mind?"

"If this is your idea of marriage counseling, you can save your breath. I need to get back to the children and I don't have time for a lecture. I know what I'm doing, Rex. Just get it over with."

"I'm sorry, Cass. I can't do it. It's not right."

"Why?" His eyes widened. "Oh. The license?" He searched through the pocket. Pulling out a piece of paper, he unfolded it and shoved it toward the judge. "I have it. Here it is!"

"I wasn't referring to the license, Cass."

"Then what?"

"You don't love her."

"How do you know?"

"My stars, man, you've already admitted you just met her today."

"That's not against the law. Plenty of men order brides they don't love, and I happen to know some marriages that have worked out very well."

The judge leaned in and lowered his voice to a whisper. "Cass, if it's a woman you want, there are discreet ways to arrange a little tete-a-tete without having to marry her. I won't pretend to know a lot about scripture, but I do remember my Granny telling me one time that the Bible says something to the effect that it's better to marry than to burn." His lip curled. "So if that's what's bothering you, I'm sure there are all sorts of mitigating circumstances that the Good Lord takes into consideration. After all, he's the one who made us, right? You may be a preacher, but you're human, like the rest of us men. So, go give that young lady a couple of dollars and bid her farewell. Come back to this room Saturday night, and everything will be set up. Nothing to worry about. You and I will be the only two privy to the arrangement—other than the woman, of course—and she has ample reason to keep her mouth shut."

Cass rolled his eyes. "Like you said, Rex, you don't know a lot about scripture. You leave the preaching to me, and you just do your job. I'm going to marry the girl. I've given her my word, so you can either make this easy—or I'll go downstairs and book her a room here at this hotel. But I *will* find someone tomorrow who'll marry us."

"No need in us standing here, arguing. Have a seat."

"Not unless you agree to marry me, and I'm in a bit of a hurry."

"Fine. I just have a few questions and if you still feel the same way after we talk, then I'll do it, against my better judgment."

Cass pulled out a chair and sat down. "Ask away."

"How old is she?"

"Almost seventeen."

He smirked. "So, the answer is sixteen?"

"Yes."

"And how old is Gazelle, now? About the same age?"

His brow furrowed. "Of course not."

"But she's a teenager, am I right?"

"No. Gazelle's a kid and you know it."

"How old?"

"Twelve."

The judge grinned. "So, what you're saying is your daughter is going on thirteen, and you're wanting to take home a sixteen-year-old as your wife."

No, Gazelle is twelve and uh, Ruby" . . ." He scratched his head. "I mean . . . Roxy." With his forefinger he swiped sweat from his upper lip. "The woman sitting out there that I plan to marry is almost seventeen."

The judge slapped his palm to his forehead. "Good grief, you don't even know her name, do you?"

"I do. I just forgot it. It's Rachel."

"Cass, I'm not sure you've noticed—since you haven't seemed to notice much—but the girl is barefoot. That tells me she comes from nothing and she's sweet-talked you into marrying her.

She's a looker, for sure, but are you so blind you can't see what she's after? Everyone in the county knows you're a wealthy man. I can't say I blame her for wanting access to a gold mine, but to marry her when you don't have to, is ludicrous. Frankly, as the old-timers say, I think you're trying to beat the devil around the stump. You and I both know you're marrying her for the same illicit reason I pretend to go on a business trip about once a month. The difference is, I don't try to convince myself I'm doing the right thing. Shucks, me and the devil have a pact. I leave him alone and he leaves me alone. You can keep chasing him, if it makes you feel better, but if you ask me, he's winning."

Cass shuddered at Rex's vulgar insinuation. He wanted to believe that in spite of the age difference his sole motivation for marrying the girl was for the sake of the children. They needed a mother. Not only that, but he sent for her and she came because he promised to marry her. Wasn't he obligated to keep his word?

Rex rambled on, but Cass paid little attention. He sat quietly, recalling a Chalkboard Lecture on Spiritual Warfare he gave a few years back in Montrose, when he warned against whipping the devil around the stump instead of planting one's feet on the solid Rock. Was he doing the very thing he preached against? Did he not pray before sending the train ticket? Of course, he did. Surely, God in His wisdom had sent exactly what he needed. Was it so terrible that she happened to be easy to look at?

Whipping the Devil around the Stump

There was no denying the girl was strikingly beautiful, even with bobbed hair and bare feet. But was it possible Rex could be right? Could Cass deny that his heart longed for her from the moment he laid eyes on her? The bitter taste of bile rose to his throat. *Sometimes even a preacher needs a preacher.* He rubbed his chin while gazing out the window. "Looks like the sun's going down and I think we've said all we need to say. We'll be leaving."

The judge shoved his chair back. "So, you won't change your mind?"

"No." He picked up his coat. "Sorry for wasting your time."

The judge threw up his hands. "I give up. Go down to the desk and ask Adrian to come up here. We'll need a witness. And tell the girl to come on in."

Cass jumped up. "Forget it. She's obviously scared and I won't have you insulting her the way you did me."

"I don't plan to question her. No need to make her lie. We both know why she wants to get married." He glanced down at the marriage license and grunted. "You said her name was Rachel." He pointed to a line on the paper. "Her name is Rebekah, Cass."

"So?" Cass lifted his shoulders in a shrug and walked out.

Forty minutes after stepping from the train, Miss Rebekah McAlister had become Mrs. Rebekah Marlowe, wife of the Reverend Castle B. Marlowe.

CHAPTER 4

The preacher held out his hand and helped Rebekah into the buggy. She thought of the many times her papa accused her of talking too much, yet now it seemed the cat had gotten her tongue. Brother Cass didn't seem to mind, though. He wasn't full of talk, himself.

After a long, torturing silence, she said, "How old is your baby?"

He smiled for the first time. "Enoch is eleven months."

"Oh."

"He's a handful. Has been since his mama passed."

Rebekah nodded as if she understood. After another long silence, she asked. "When did she, uh . . . you know . . .pass?"

His eyes glassed over. "Ten months, one week . . ." He rubbed his chin. His gaze shot upward as if the precise answer could he found in the clouds. "And two days."

"I'm sorry for your loss." She licked her dry lips. At least, they were now conversing. "I'm sure it's been very difficult for you, especially with a baby. I love little babies and I can handle most all the chores around a place while you're on your trips. I reckon I can do most anything a man can do. . I'm used to hard work and I'm a pretty good carpenter. I practically built our barn by myself." Remembering how her papa accused her of rattling off at the mouth, she clamped her lips together.

"Thank you, but those skills won't be necessary. I have a barn. I'm sure you'll do fine."

Replaying her lengthy monologue in her head, she grimaced, but her fears eased, when he spoke in a calming voice.

"I had an elderly widowed aunt who moved in with us before my wife died, but unfortunately, Aunt Jewel passed away last month. I thought I could manage alone, but I realize that my children and my ministry are both suffering. I can't keep up this pace much longer."

"How did . . . never mind. None of my business."

Though she didn't ask how his wife died, the preacher seemed to read her mind. Looking straight ahead, he mumbled. "Drowned. She drowned."

Her mouth gaped open "Oh, m'goodness. I'm so sorry. I'm sure you miss her very much."

Seeing the moisture in his eyes caused her to quickly change the subject. "I love babies, but I said that already, didn't I? I'm sure little Enoch and I will get along just fine."

In a voice hardly audible, he said, "My little Gopher is not my only concern. Honestly, I worry more about the others."

The compassion, which had swelled up unexpectedly inside Rebekah's soft heart, quickly diminished. Was he saying he cared more for the parishioners on his circuit than he did for his own motherless baby? Maybe he wasn't so different from her papa, after all. She'd always believed her father would choose anyone over her, but she expected more of a preacher. Maybe Aunt Nellie didn't know him as well as she thought she did.

He pulled the buggy up in front of a beautiful rambling two-story house and stopped. A coral vine laden with bright pink flowers trailed up one of the many fluted columns surrounding the huge wrap around porch. Rebekah had read of mansions in her books, but even in her wildest imagination, she'd never been capable of conjuring up such a magnificent setting.

Her eyes widened. "My goodness, wouldja look at that? Without a doubt, this is the most beautiful house I've ever laid eyes on. Looks like a castle, doesn't it? Appears to be made out of some sort of precious stone with little diamonds imbedded in it, the way it glistens when the sun hits it. Reckon what it's made of, Preacher?"

He smiled, which caused Rebekah to squirm. Did he think her ignorant for asking such a question?

"It's marble, hauled in from a quarry at a place called Tate, Georgia."

Her slumped shoulders lifted. "Marble? You don't say. Do you happen to know the people who live here?"

His dark eyes lit up when he quipped, "Intimately."

"Goodness, gracious, I suppose they must be about the richest folks in the whole wide world. Thank you for showing it to me. I Suwannee, it's a site to behold."

Before he could respond, the door to the house opened and children came rushing toward the buggy.

Rebekah counted five as they swarmed around the preacher. From the smile stretched across the Reverend's lips, it was plain to see he was fond of children. He jumped out of the buggy and as they tugged on his coattail, he patted each head, gave hugs, then walked around to the other side.

Standing in front of her, he extended his hand to help lift her off. He looked so refined in his black suit, white shirt and narrow tie. A dark curl fell between his eyes. She'd not noticed until now how extremely handsome he was. Not that it made any difference to her.

"Welcome to Amelia House, Rebekah."

Amelia's house? Maybe he didn't pay attention to her bare feet, but she recalled how the judge had sneered. Rebekah was sure his rich friend, Amelia would have the same reaction, especially after she learned the preacher had married her. With her hand cupped over her mouth, she whispered, "If it ain't asking too much, I'd like to go. I don't want to get out here."

He cocked his head and with beady eyes, glared as if she'd blurted out a swear word.

"I'm sorry you don't approve, but this is where I live. Where *we* live."

Her jaw dropped. "You mean . . .?"

A little girl who appeared to be four or five years old gazed at Rebekah. "Father, is this our new mother?"

Father? Rebekah found the words hard to swallow. *Their mother? All five of them?*

Brother Cass nodded, smiled at the child, then took the baby from the arms of the oldest boy. "Kids, this is Rebekah and she's my new wife, which makes her your stepmother, so I expect you to treat her with the utmost respect, by honoring and obeying as if she'd given birth to you. Understand?"

Perhaps *they* understood, but not Rebekah.

The chatter stopped and the silence was more frightening than the noise, as ten wide eyes stared in her direction. Though they nodded in unison, Rebekah was sure it was confirmation they understood English—not an agreement to abide by their father's request.

The little tow-headed girl seemed puzzled. "You married a stepmother, Father?"

The oldest girl grunted. "Yeah, like in Cinderella. You remember that story, don't you?"

Rebekah's throat tightened. In her dreams, she'd always been the beloved Cinderella—not even in her worst nightmares was she ever the wicked stepmother. Her only hope was that she'd soon wake up.

The preacher chuckled and remarked, "Not that kind of

stepmother," though neither Rebekah nor the children laughed with him.

Then, tapping each child on the head, one by one, the preacher made the introductions. "This is Eli, he's eleven and answers to Goat." He smiled. "Trust me, you don't want to buck heads with him. He can win any argument." The preacher tousled the tall, lanky kid's hair with his hand, then turned his attention to a pouty blonde, blue-eyed girl. "Meet Esther. This little queen is twelve but thinks she twenty. We call her Gazelle and it fits her well, since she can outrun any boy in the county."

From the girl's icy stare, Rebekah had a feeling the queen wasn't open to the idea of a foreigner invading her palace.

"Elkanah and Elizabeth here are twins, though any similarities are hard to find. They're five and answer to Goose and Gander. Gander paddles through life with ease but Goose is shy and tends to get her feathers ruffled rather easily."

They were all cute kids, but their cold stares told her they were as unsure of her as she was of them. The preacher drew the baby close to his face and kissed his rosy cheek. "And this is my wee little Gopher, whose proper name is Enoch. And as Enoch of old experienced a transformation, so shall our little man soon be changed. Right, Gazelle?"

Gazelle hadn't taken her eyes off Rebekah's feet. "I think your wife may be the one in need of a translation, Father. I'll wager she has no clue who Enoch is in the Bible, do you?"

"Watch your language, daughter. We shall have no wagering

in this household. Now, please take your brother in the house and change him."

She rolled her eyes. "You said you were gonna get us a new mother to help with chores and to take care of Gopher. Why can't she change him?"

Rebekah's voice quaked. "Of course. I can do that."

The Preacher shook his head. "Thank you, but Gazelle must do as she's told." He handed the baby to the pouty girl and said, "Rebekah will be a big help to us all, but she's been on a long trip and I'm sure she's exhausted."

Rebekah blotted the sweat from her upper lip. *They hate me.* For the first time in her life, home with Papa was looking better than it ever had. The children all ran into the house, as if they felt the need to escape the wicked stepmother their father had brought home.

CHAPTER 5

The preacher's handsome face pinched into a frown. "You really didn't know, did you? About the children, I mean? I can't believe your aunt would've failed to mention it. I'm so sorry. I had no idea."

The tears she'd managed to hide trailed down her cheeks. "Aunt Nellie said you had a baby yet she never mentioned the others." *The others?* It suddenly dawned on her that the preacher wasn't referring to the parishioners when he stated the baby wasn't his only concern, but he was concerned for the *others*. After meeting the little fireball, Gazelle, Rebekah determined he had plenty of reason to worry.

Drawing a handkerchief from his coat pocket, he blotted her cheek as a tear made its way down her face. "Please don't cry. You don't have to stay. I'm afraid in my desperation, I wasn't thinking straight. Rex was right. You're a mere kid, yourself."

Rebekah bristled. She was ready to leave—until he added the last sentence. How dare he call her a kid. She'd been a woman since she was thirteen years old. There was nothing a thirty-year-old female could do that she couldn't do as well, except maybe cook, but she was quite sure no woman could've cooked anything to satisfy Papa.

"You're wrong. I'm not a kid and I'll prove it to you." She couldn't deny she was scared. But wouldn't any woman be a little frightened at having five children unexpectedly thrust upon her to raise? Of course, they would. Besides, she had nowhere to go. Papa wouldn't let her come back, even if she wanted to.

From the preacher's troubled expression, Rebekah gathered he was as unsure about the arrangement as she was. He was looking for a wife but concluded he'd brought home another child. She'd prove to him he married a woman. Plenty of women married at sixteen and in a few months, she'd turn seventeen.

He pursed his lips. "Am I understanding you correctly? You're willing to stay and take on such a huge responsibility?"

Swallowing the lump in her throat, she stiffened. "Yessir. I'll do it."

She remembered him saying those same words to Aunt Nellie. Didn't he have as much, if not more reason to be frightened of such an arrangement? Surely, it wasn't easy for him to take in a stranger, not knowing whether he was making the right decision for his children. How could either of them know, for sure?

He escorted her into the house, and the children kept their distance, eyeing her as if she were a dangerous animal to be kept at bay. The beautifully furnished parlor was much larger than the tiny cabin she'd shared with her father. Velvet drapes matching the furniture hung from the high ceilings and draped in folds on the polished floors. The humongous fireplace was constructed of the same marble as the exterior of the house and the mantle had an assortment of pictures of the preacher with his arm around a beautiful woman. Over the sofa was an oil painting of the same woman in a wedding gown.

It suddenly became clear to her why Brother Cass didn't care what she looked like. There was no woman alive who could measure up to his deceased wife.

Gazelle walked in, holding the baby and pointed to the painting. "That was our mother. Beautiful, wasn't she?"

Rebekah nodded. "Very beautiful."

"She and father fell in love when they weren't much older than me. Isn't that true, father?"

"Yes, Gazelle. That's true, sweetheart." He changed the subject. "Have you children had supper?"

Gazelle nodded. "We had a delicious supper. The widow Matthews brought a ham pie and a blueberry cobbler. It was much better than the rice pudding Miss Lowder brought last week. The widow Matthews said to be sure and tell you she was sorry she missed you. When I told her you went to get married, she just laughed. I don't think she believed me."

His brow formed a vee. "Gazelle, why don't you fix a bottle for Gopher and put him to bed. He's falling asleep on your shoulder."

Gazelle cocked her head and smiled. "I'll be happy to father. I love rocking him to sleep, but maybe his stepmother might like to do the honors. It would be a good way for them to bond."

Rebekah nodded. "I think she's right." Maybe she'd misjudged the girl. "Thank you, Gazelle." With her hands cupped under his little arms, she tugged, yet felt Gazelle tightening her hold on him, refusing to let go. Feeling the tug, he opened his eyes, his back arched and his whole body stiffened. He flung his hands around Gazelle's neck and screamed.

Gazelle gave a little tsk-tsk. "Bless his little heart, he's terrified of you. Maybe it wasn't such a good idea, after all."

Brother Cass said, "I'm sorry, Rebekah, but I'm sure he'll warm up to you in time. Shall we finish the tour?"

It wasn't the baby who worried her most. It was the manipulative, spiteful big sister. This was going to be a difficult situation, if not impossible.

He led her through the French Doors. "And this is the dining room."

The dining room was as large as the parlor with the longest table Rebekah had ever seen. She counted nine chairs on either side, with one on each end. Who needs a table large enough for twenty people? *The Preacher?* She bit her bottom lip to stop the quivering. As long as she could remember, Rebekah dreamed of having a large family, but she dismissed that idea the moment five children came running toward the buggy.

There was a butler's pantry separating it from the kitchen. The back door led out to a wrap-around porch and overlooked a beautiful pasture, a hog pen and a handsome red barn. Even the barn was nicer than the house back home. Brother Cass said, "It's Goat's responsibility to feed the hogs and Gazelle does the milking. However, you might consider relieving her in the mornings. It's not so bad now that school is not in session, but it's been difficult for her to get up several times in the night with Gopher, to be ready to milk at daylight, then get to school on time. When her grades dropped, the school master complained she was falling asleep in class."

Now was not the time to let him know she'd never milked a cow in her life. Papa bought their milk from Widow Jennings. But how hard could it be?

He led her down a long hall that had a beautiful canopy bed. "This is our bedroom." He coughed in his hand. "I meant it was mine and Amelia's bedroom. We were married fourteen years and it's still difficult not to think of myself as a married man."

She wanted to remind him that he *was* a married man, but it was hard to believe he could forget. She hadn't forgotten for a single moment from the time they left the hotel.

Goose, the five-year-old twin had followed quietly on their heels. "You can sleep in the girls' room with Gazelle and me."

He glanced at Rebekah, then quickly looked away. "Honey, it's true that Rebekah is younger than your mother was, but I want you to understand she's not a girl. She's a woman and as such, we shall allow her to choose where she shall sleep."

Rebekah tried to read between the lines, but there was too much white space. What was he saying? There was only one thing she knew for sure—she would *not* be sleeping in Gazelle's room. She'd be afraid to close her eyes all night. However, adorable little Goose was worming her way into Rebekah's heart. What a sweet kid and it was apparent she longed for attention.

Goose pointed to a door across from the Master bedroom and announced quite enthusiastically, "That's my Mother's room."

A blush painted the preacher's face. As if he needed to explain, he said, "Amelia moved into the guest room after she became pregnant with Gopher. She was very sick while carrying the child and insisted she didn't want to keep me up at night." He turned his head but not before she saw the moisture in his eyes. He mumbled, "She was thoughtful that way."

Goose said, "Since you'll be taking Mother's place, do you want to sleep in her room?"

Brother Cass quickly spoke up. "Perhaps I should explain something, Goose. I don't want you to think of Rebekah as taking your Mother's place."

"But I thought—"

He knelt beside the child and held her hands in his. "I know this is a bit confusing. I'll try to explain Rebekah's place in the household. You know when Mr. Hill was sick and had to be away from school for a while? Was he still your teacher, even though he was away?"

The child nodded with a smile as if she understood. "Yessir.

But Miss Annie filled in while Mr. Hill was in the hospital."

"That's right. Miss Annie didn't take Mr. Hill's place. He was still your teacher, but Miss Annie was a substitute, which means she was there to see that you children continued to receive an education. She did some things the way Mr. Hill had done them, but she also incorporated her own style of teaching. Yet, even though Miss Annie came in to help, you'll always remember Mr. Hill as your teacher at Vinegar Bend School. Do you understand what I'm trying to say?"

"I think so. You brought her here to help until Mother comes back."

Rebekah heard footsteps and glanced behind her in time to see eleven-year-old Goat rolling his eyes.

Doing nothing to hide his disgust, he grumbled, "Use your noggin for something besides a hat rack, Goose! Mother isn't ever coming back." His voice rose a pitch. "Not ever. Do you understand? Never."

His little sister's bottom lip quivered. "But I thought Father said—"

"I know what you thought but that was a bunch of horse feathers. Mother is in heaven and nobody comes back once they go to heaven." He glared at Cass. "Tell her, Father. Tell her the truth." His words spat out so fast, Rebekah had trouble following.

Cass's face turned a bright shade of red, whether from embarrassment or anger Rebekah couldn't discern.

His voice was low and contained. "Goat, I'll concede the

analogy I used was a poor one, but your crude remarks were out of line and I cannot—will not—tolerate such insolence. Do you understand?"

Goat lowered his head and mumbled, "Sorry, Father. I just didn't think it was right to leave Goose expecting Mother to come back."

Cass ran his fingers through his son's hair. "Well, if she was confused, I think you've made it quite plain. Am I right Goose? Do you understand?"

She nodded. "Yessir. But how long will our stepmother be here?"

Her older brother, sounding even more perturbed than before, threw his arms in the air. "What a silly question, Goose. Father married her."

"I know that."

"Well, then you should also know she'll be living here until she dies and goes to heaven."

The preacher grinned, although Rebekah wasn't sure why.

He said, "Well, Goat, since Rebekah is a mite younger than I, there's always the possibility I could enter heaven's gates first. If that should happen, it gives me great comfort to know you children would not be sent to an orphanage. Rebekah would be here for you."

Gazelle stood in the doorway, holding little Gopher. The coldness in her voice brought a sudden chill to the room. "If you die, Father and that girl stays here, I'll tell you right now I'll leave home. I told you I didn't want a stepmother. You just married her because she's pretty."

His eyes darkened. "Gazelle, please hand Gopher to me and go to your room. You can begin memorizing the thirteenth Chapter of Corinthians, and when you're ready to recite it, you may come down."

She bounded up the stairs in a huff.

"Pardon my daughter's rude behavior. She wasn't like this until after her Mother died." He opened the door across the hall, nodded his head in the direction of the high poster bed, then promptly closed it. As if he needed to confirm what he'd already stated, he simply muttered, "The guest room."

Rebekah hadn't noticed until now that the children were no longer following them. As much as it hurt to say it, there was no denying the truth. "Brother Cass, I'm afraid we've made a terrible mistake."

He glared into her eyes. "First let's get one thing straight. I'm known as Brother Cass to the parishioners. As your husband, you will refer to me as Cass. And these children have been without a woman's guidance far too long. I buried myself in grief and haven't been the disciplinarian I needed to be. As a result, they've become a bit rebellious, but I promise to step up and work with you to get them under control."

"But don't you see? They hate me, and I don't think that will ever change, especially if I'm responsible for correcting their behavior."

His jaw flexed. "Perhaps you're right. I can see this is a job for a more mature person. Since you'll be leaving, there's no need to tour the upstairs. You may put your bag in the guest room, and I'll put you on the train first thing in the morning for the destination of your choice. It will be a minor effort to have the marriage annulled, since . . ." He looked away. "Well, I'm just saying it will be no trouble at all. I'll take care of it. Now, if you'll excuse me, I need to go up and see that the children are all tucked in. Goodnight, Rebekah."

The lump in her throat almost choked her. "Goodnight, Brother Cass."

CHAPTER 6

Rebekah closed the door to the Guest Room and tightened her hand over her mouth to silence the sobs trying to make their way out. She didn't want to leave. Why did she have to say they'd made a terrible mistake? The real mistake was in voicing her concerns aloud without weighing the consequences. Sure, she was frightened, considering she had no experience at being a wife or a mother. But being forced out with nowhere to go frightened her much more than Gazelle's irritating provocation.

She placed her carpetbag on the thick, fluffy mattress and pulled out her nightgown. Tears flowed from her eyes as her gaze darted about the room at the crystal gaslights hanging from the ceiling to the gorgeous walnut armoire, to the dressing table with tri-fold mirror, to the huge carved posters on the bed. She wanted to preserve every magnificent detail in her memory. Even with an enormous imagination such as hers, there was no way to conjure up such splendor.

Just as she crawled under the sheets, she heard the baby let out a blood-curdling scream. Three hours later, the grandfather clock in the hall struck eleven times and Gopher was still crying. The sound of heavy footsteps pacing back and forth across the wood floors in the room across the hall brought tears to her eyes. *Cass must be exhausted.* She had a sinking feeling inside her stomach. Until now, she'd only thought of him as "the preacher." But he was more than that. Much more. He was everything any woman could want in a man. Her throat tightened. Yes . . . *any* woman, including her. So why was she so careless with her words?

She awoke the next morning and heard voices in the kitchen. After dressing, she grabbed her carpetbag, then hurried down the long hall to find Cass standing over the stove. The pungent smell of salt pork filled her nostrils.

Gazelle was in a rather jovial mood, chatting nonstop as she set the table.

Rebekah coughed in her hand in an effort to be noticed. "Good Morning."

Obviously displeased that her lengthy monologue had been interrupted, Gazelle's disapproval was evident by her poked-out lip.

Without turning around, Cass continued to fry the meat. "This is the day the Lord hath made. We shall rejoice and be glad in it."

Rebekah got the point. So, he was glad, was he? Well, she could stop punishing herself for saying the marriage was a mistake because obviously he was ready to have it dissolved before she opened her mouth. She'd merely given him an excuse to get rid of her.

"Can I help?"

Gazelle's bubbly attitude suddenly dissolved. "No. Father and I are a team. We don't need anyone helping us. Right, Father?"

Rebekah bit her lip. Apparently, Cass had already given his daughter the news that she wanted to hear.

Cass muttered. "I think we can manage, thank you. Have a seat. You should eat a hearty breakfast, since the train trip will be long."

"I'm not hungry. Really."

"Maybe not now, but you will be."

Cass said, "Gazelle, go tell your brothers and sister to come to the table, but please do it quietly, and don't wake little Gopher. He barely closed his eyes last night."

She bounded up a flight of stairs, and could be heard yelling, "Breakfast is ready. Come on down."

Cass cringed, but said nothing as he waited for everyone to take their place. Then turning to Rebekah, he said, "Please have a seat and eat."

Not wanting to cause more chaos, she nodded. When she walked up to the table, Cass pulled out a chair for her. The lump in her throat grew. Such a gentleman, despite the trouble she'd caused him.

Gazelle frowned. "Not there, Father! That's Mother's place."

Cass chewed on the inside of his cheek. "Then suppose you sit here, Gazelle, and Rebekah shall sit in your chair."

"Why should I have to change places?"

Rebekah stepped back. "You shouldn't, Gazelle. No need for anyone to give up their seat for me. Please enjoy your breakfast." She reached down and picked up her carpet bag from off the floor.

Goose's eyes widened. "Where are you going, Rebekah?"

Rebekah glanced at Cass, then patted Goose on the head. "Since I'm not hungry, I think I shall go sit in the buggy and enjoy the beautiful sunrise." Though it should be of no concern to her, she did wonder why with all his money—and it was evident, he was quite wealthy—he'd be riding around on a one-horse buggy when he could afford a new automobile.

Chairs rumbled as the children took their seats at the table.

Goose said, "But why do you have your . . . "

Cass bellowed. "Quiet, Goose, while I ask God's blessings on our food." All heads were bowed as Cass prayed. Rebekah tiptoed out, hoping to avoid further questions.

Sitting in the buggy, her eyes glazed over as she took in the splendor from the vast cottonfields just coming into bloom in the distance, to the freshly painted white fence surrounding the horse farm across the road. Her gaze lingered on the magnificent structure, Cass called, The Amelia House. But as splendid as it all was, the grandest of all was not the pastures, the horses nor the magnificent structure, but the real beauty resided on the inside— the kind, Godly man who was so desperate, he agreed to marry her, sight unseen. If only she could've been what he needed.

Minutes later, Cass came walking out the door, holding a stylish pair of women's button-up boots. He laid them in her lap. "I have no use for these. Thought you might could wear them. You have a small foot like—" He stopped.

Rebekah cleared her throat and sat up straight, determined not to cry. They were the most beautiful shoes she'd ever seen. "Thank you. They're lovely." She could hardly wait to try them on but determined it wouldn't be proper in front of the preacher, even if they were married.

He mumbled as he pointed toward dark clouds above. "Looks like rain's coming this way, but you should be home before nightfall."

No way could she return home. There had to be another solution . . . something besides working in a saloon. She swallowed hard. What was she thinking? Being choosy was not an option. She'd take whatever she could find and if it happened to be dancing around in a scantily clad costume in a bar full of drunken men, then so be it. Anything would be better than returning to face her Papa.

Rebekah tried desperately to think of something to say as they rode toward town. "Uh . . . Prea . . . I mean, Cass . . . I suppose you won't be back on the circuit until you find someone to care for the children while you're away?"

His eyes darkened and he glared as if she'd slapped him in the face. His voice sounded stoic. "Please don't feel it your concern. I managed before you came, and I'll manage without you." He popped the whip in the air. The horse understood his cue and upped the pace.

Rebekah understood her cue as well. Without saying a word, he had made it perfectly clear that he nor his children should concern her. But he was wrong. She *was* concerned. It was too much responsibility to put on Gazelle. No wonder the kid was bitter, with such high expectations placed on her young shoulders.

Her mind was still wandering when the buggy suddenly came to a halt and she realized they were stopped in view of the train depot. She glanced at the boots in her lap.

His voice quaked. "I'll turn my head, if you'd like to put them on. You'll find a pair of stockings inside the shoes."

Her heart pounded. She could hardly wait to see them on her feet. "Thank you, Cass. I'd like that." After buttoning the last button, she held her legs straight out, to admire the beautiful boots.

"Cass, you can look now. They're perfect."

Even if she had planned to go home, which she hadn't . . . but even if she had, she couldn't now. Papa would beat the living tar out of her if he knew she'd allowed someone to give her shoes. The church women had offered to give her a dress last year, but Papa insisted they didn't take charity.

Cass clicked his tongue and the horse galloped off and stopped in front of the depot. He jumped out, rushed around to her side, and lifted her from the buggy. He reached in his pocket and pulled out folded bills. "Here. There's enough to buy your ticket home and a little to help you get on your feet."

Until now, she hadn't even thought about how she would buy a ticket, even if she wanted to go home. She had no right to accept anything else from him and wanted to refuse, but out of desperation, swallowed her pride and thanked him. "One day, I'll pay you back. I don't know how long it will take, but you'll see. I'll pay back every penny and that's a promise."

"It's a gift, Rebekah. You don't pay for gifts. I'm sorry you came under the false impression that things would be easy. Nellie should have told you about the children—*all* of the children—and saved you the trouble of coming."

He walked her to the ticket window. She stalled and stepped back, allowing the family behind her to go next. In a low voice, she said, "Cass, it's good you can have the marriage dissolved so you'll be free to find someone suitable. You need help for sure. I just wish I could've been the one."

He glanced away. "Yeah. Me, too." He reached out and shook her hand. "You'd better get your ticket. The train should be here soon. Goodbye, Rebekah."

If she said another word, she might end up boo-hooing. With a plastered smile, she blinked away the tears trying to escape and with a slight wave of her hand, she watched as he rode out of sight.

The man at the window said, "Ma'am, where to?"

"Pardon?"

Then, realizing he was waiting for her to purchase a ticket, she shook her head. "Nowhere."

"Are you waiting for someone?"

"No sir. Not waiting on nobody." Rebekah turned and walked away, mulling over her answer. Nowhere was exactly where she was headed, and there was no one who cared enough to come looking for her.

CHAPTER 7

Rebekah followed the tracks back to town, where she remembered seeing a help-wanted sign in front of a ladies' dress shop on the way to the depot. She had difficulty seeing where she was going, with her gaze focused on her feet. A tinge of guilt snuck up on her.

Was it disrespectful to wear Cass's poor departed wife's beautiful boots? But the guilt was short-lived, overridden by a stronger sense of pride. She had shoes. Beautiful, black and white, button up boots, and the fit was perfect.

Rebekah walked past the Watering Hole Saloon and the snooty lady's degrading words came back to her, causing a sickening ache in her stomach. *"I make judgments based on what I see, and I have no idea if you can sing. But it's my understanding that chorus girls don't have to carry a tune if they're pretty to look at and can prance around on a stage. You certainly fit the description. . . especially with that bobbed haircut."* She reached up and tugged on her hair. She'd almost forgotten how short it was. Cass didn't seem to mind, but then he wasn't concerned with how she looked—only if she could keep house, cook, and care for the children. Being a man of the cloth, he couldn't afford to have a live-in maid, and with no thoughts of falling in love again, he would've married the woman who showed up on his doorstep. In fact, that's essentially what he did. Didn't he understand what he had to offer a woman? Any woman would be crazy not to fall in love with such a handsome, kind, compassionate man.

Rebekah stopped in front of Elsie's Millinery Shop, straightened her bodice and sucked in a deep breath. Her heart sank to her stomach when she realized the Help Wanted sign she'd seen on the way in, was no longer in the window. With her shoulders slung back, feigning confidence, she strode inside.

An attractive older lady, although a mite on the heavy side, met her with a warm smile. "Come in, sugar. How can I help you, today?"

"I recollect seeing a Help Wanted sign in the window earlier, but I see it's gone. This is a mighty pretty store, and if you'd be obliged to hire me to work here. I'd work hard. Really hard." Her eyes squinted, as she tried to analyze the woman's peculiar expression.

"Sweetheart, I had to remove the sign, when I realized I couldn't afford to hire anyone. But you might try Wink's Grocery across the street. You must be new in town. I don't recollect seeing you around Vinegar Bend before."

Rebekah tried to hide her disappointment. Working in such a fine shop and helping women try on the pretty hats would've been wonderful. "Yes'm. I just got into town."

"Where are you from, sugar?"

"North Alabama, ma'am. Up about Sipsey Ridge in a little community called New Hope."

"New Hope! Well, I declare, that sounds like a fine place to live. We can all use hope, can't we? And to live in a place that promises a fresh, new hope—well, that just makes you feel warm all over, doesn't it?"

Rebekah forced a smile. There was no reason to explain the utter hopelessness she felt while living in a place she privately referred to as No-Hope. Nor how with a few careless words, she blew the only chance of hope she'd ever had, when she confessed to Cass the marriage was too difficult a task for her to undertake. If only—

The woman held out her hand. "My name is Elsie. Elsie Drummond. And you are—?"

"Rebekah, ma'am. I'm Rebekah McAlister, Mrs. Drummond."

"That would be Miss, not Mrs., dear. But please, call me Elsie. Everyone else in town does."

"Yes'm. Thank you, Miz Elsie"

"Well, welcome to Vinegar Bend, dear." She dropped her gaze. "Oh, my, what lovely boots. I recall having a pair in the store, about a year ago, exactly like those. I ordered them special for Mrs. Marlowe, God rest her soul. Died a tragic death, shortly after her last baby was born, but then you'd have no way of knowing." She popped her palm to her forehead. "Oh, dear, how I do go on. I didn't mean to bring up the town gossip, but it was seeing your boots that caused my mind to wander." Her head cocked to the side. "I don't suppose you were related to Amelia—Mrs. Marlowe?"

Rebekah shook her head. "No ma'am."

"Seeing the boots, I thought maybe—" She lifted a shoulder in a shrug. "Well, of course, you wouldn't be related."

Although Rebekah wanted to know why she would make such a statement, she was more interested in knowing what she meant by 'town gossip?' Surely, it was a careless choice of words. Admittedly, Rebekah had only known Cass for a very short while, but there was no doubt in her mind that no one would ever have cause to gossip about such a fine man nor his beautiful wife. She thanked her and was walking out the door, when Miss Elsie called her.

"Wait, dear. Maybe, we can work out something."

She stopped in her tracks. "Really? You mean it?"

"I said maybe. Can you sew?"

Rebekah hung her head. She knew it was too good to be true. "I'm afraid not. At least not well enough to make pretty dresses like you sell, here. I didn't grow up with a mama, so the only sewing I do, I taught myself."

"But you can thread a needle, right?"

She giggled. "Yes'm, I can do that."

"Then, I can teach you what you need to know. I make the dresses, but I could use someone to make hats. I can fill the dress orders, but it's difficult keeping up with the millinery orders."

"I wish I could say I could do that, but truth is, I think making a hat would be a whole lot harder than making a dress."

"Horsefeathers. I have a feeling you're very smart and can catch on quickly. There are only a few basic styles, but it's the icing on the cake that makes each one distinct."

"Icing? Cake?"

Elsie laughed. "That's what I call the frills—you know—the netting, lace, ribbons and feathers."

"And you really think you can teach me?"

"I have no doubt. But I'll tell you upfront, I can't afford to pay much. Papa died and left a bank note on the homeplace and I'm determined to pay it off. Although I have more business than I can take in, there isn't much money left at the end of the month, after paying the bank. Where are you staying?"

"Uh . . . I just got into town and haven't had opportunity to look for a place, yet."

"Perfect. I have a room upstairs, if you'd like to stay here. Perhaps we could count it as part of your pay?"

Rebekah's heart fluttered. "Yes'm, I'd like that. I'm very grateful, ma'am."

"You can move in today, get settled and I'll begin teaching you tomorrow. Where are your clothes?"

Holding the carpetbag in front of her, she timidly responded, "They're in my bag."

The lines on Miss Elsie's forehead made Rebekah think she might renege on her offer. Instead, she rubbed her hand across the back of her neck, and said, "I see. Well, the furnishings aren't fine, but at least you'll have a bed, a pump, a toilet and a washtub for your baths. It's where the previous owner of the store lived, but I only use it for storage. I've continued to live in the house down the street, where I was raised."

****

Cass walked across the pasture and sat on a stump, where he often went to be alone with the Lord. Some of his best sermon ideas came when he sat still and listened—the two things he found virtually impossible to do while in the house with five children all vying for his attention. But today, he wasn't preparing a sermon. He reached in his coat pocket and pulled out a letter he picked up in the mornings mail. His throat constricted. Carefully, unfolding the letter, he read the lines that he could now quote from memory.

Dear Cass,

Well, I can only imagine your shock to learn that I am indeed alive and well. I have attempted to write you several times, but there seemed no way I could adequately explain why I had to do what I did, but I now have a compelling reason to attempt this difficult letter.

Ashamed to admit to you that I scrupulously planned my demise, I considered insisting I was knocked out and lost my memory—or that I was kidnapped, or that—well, you get the picture. But you always knew when I was lying. The truth is, I married you because you are the best-looking man on the Planet, and I'm a very vain woman. I liked showing you off.

I've always wanted the best of everything, and I knew I had the best with you, but I learned quickly I was not cut out to be a Preacher's wife or a mother. After the baby was born, I realized I cared more about me than I did the five children I bore you. That confession sounds cold, but you and I both know it's the truth. Cass, for years, I wanted out, but I cared for you too much to ruin your ministry by asking you for a divorce. I suppose there's a little good in the worst of us. But now things have changed, and I feel it only fair to tell you what happened, though it pains me to admit— even to myself—what a bad person I am.

I planned this for months in advance and had secretly been stashing away cash, knowing I would need the money. You were always generous and never questioned the withdrawals. I ordered two straw hats from a mail-order catalog, and after you left, I told Bertha, the town gossip, that I was meeting an old friend at the train station. I told her we planned to take a boat ride down the Escatawpa River and picnic on the island. I knew she'd be more than happy to spread the false story, giving credence to my death. I left Aunt Jewel with the young'uns—and to make it more believable—told her I'd be bringing a guest home for supper.

I packed a bag and snuck it on the buggy, along with the two straw hats. I went down to the river and took our boat. Then several miles down stream, I tossed the hats and continued until I reached Pascagoula. At nightfall, I paddled to shore, then shoved the boat back into the water. With my bag in hand, I walked the train tracks to the nearest depot, where I bought a ticket to New

Orleans. I can't explain the eerie feeling that came over me when I read about my tragic drowning a few days later in the newspaper. It was a perfect plan. I was finally free from the shackles binding me, and I'd been able to pull it off without harming your ministry.

Cass, I know you loved me and I thought it would be easier for you to think of me as dead, rather than know the truth, but I can no longer hide it. I've found someone who wants the same things from life that I want. He's not Mr. Perfect, like you, but he's a wealthy man and can support me in the fashion to which I have become accustomed. We're perfect for one another and he wants to marry me, but he refuses unless I present a writ of divorcement.

Therefore, I'm enclosing divorce papers, and I'm sure you'll have no problem signing them. Please mail papers to the Goldwing Riverboat Casino, 2284 Waterford Walk, New Orleans, c/o Owner. No one need know I'm alive, and I say that not for my sake, but yours. It's better for your flock to continue believing your loving wife drowned than discover you're a divorced man.

Well, there's nothing more to say, dear one, except I'm truly sorry for the pain I have put you through. You didn't deserve it, but I was already drowning in boredom and had to find a way out. I'm convinced I made the right decision for both our sakes.

Sincerely,
Amelia

CHAPTER 8

After all the tears he had shed in the past year, Cass had no tears left. What kind of mother could abandon her children, then brazenly admit she loved herself more than these five beautiful little ones? Looking back, the evidence was overwhelming, though he hadn't wanted to believe it could be true.

Still sitting on the stump, he bent down, and with his hands he dug in the soft, black dirt, until he had dug a hole approximately six inches deep. Without a burial it had been difficult to have closure. Now, it was time to bury the past. Could the pain of discovering his adulterous wife's deceit be any less painful than believing she was dead? He stuck the letter and divorce papers back into his coat pocket. Then pulling out a chain with a gold watch attached, he turned it over and read the inscription on the back for the last time: *"To Cass, my first and last love, Yours forever, Amelia."* Cass quoted a scripture, then held out the watch in the palm of his hand and bowed his head. "Father in Heaven, this watch, signifies time. And it's time for casting down vain imaginations of what was, what is and what might've been. Amen." He dropped it in the hole and covered it with dirt. "Goodbye, Amelia."

He trudged back toward the house, singing the words to Rescue the Perishing.

"Down in the human heart crushed by the tempter,

Feelings lie buried that only grace can restore."

Walking into his office, he took the phone from the cradle on the wall and called Grover, a brother to one of the elders from Citronelle.

Grover answered with "Grover's Mercantile, how can I help you?"

"Grover, Castle Marlowe, here."

"Morning, preacher. To what do I owe this privilege?"

Elsie from the Dress Shoppe cut in. "Hello, Cass. I hope you and the kids are doing well."

"Very well, thank you."

Grover said, "Hang up, Elsie. He's calling me."

"Don't be so ornery, Grover. I just wanted to let him know I'm still praying for him and the young'uns."

"Fine. Now hang up."

There was a click and Grover said, "I Suwannee, I'd rather be on the party line with fifty people, than to have Elsie Drummond on the same line with me. I know I should have more patience, her being an old maid. I'm sure she gets lonely, God bless her."

"Grover, I'm calling to . . ."

"She's not a bad-looking woman. Reckon why a woman like her—you know what I mean? She appears to be right smart, the way she runs that business of hers. It don't make a lick o' sense why some fellow hasn't snatched her up. Wilma says she believes some man broke Elsie's heart and she's never wanted to fall in love again. You reckon there's something to that?"

"I'm sure she's content with her life, Grover. But I didn't call to discuss Elsie." He hoped he hadn't sounded rude, but he was in no mood to discuss Elsie Drummond.

"Sorry. I just never have been able to figure her out, but then who can understand the mind of a woman?" He cackled, then said, "But you best state your, business, preacher, before she decides she left out something and picks up again."

Cass blew out a heavy breath, then said, "Grover, I won't be going to Citronelle Wednesday evening, and if you could kindly pass the word on to your brother, I'd be obliged."

"Well, Carter will hate to hear that. The folks sure do enjoy your schoolhouse lectures, but I'll be going that way after work to see about Mama, and I'll let Carter know."

"Thanks. I know you usually try to go home at the end of the week."

"I do. Are the chil'un sick?"

"No, they're all quite well. It's . . . well, there are things at home I need to take care of. To tell the truth, I don't know when I'll be able to return. Please ask Carter to make my apologies to the group."

"You bet. We'll keep you in our prayers, preacher, and I hope whatever it is that's keeping you away will soon be settled."

He hung up, then pulled the envelope from his pocket. Letting Amelia go was the easy part. Signing a writ of divorcement was much harder.

He picked up the phone to call his mentor, Brother Angus, the old preacher who led him to the Lord when he was nineteen years old. Cass felt ashamed that he hadn't checked on the old fellow in months—wasn't even sure if he was still alive.

Sucking in a deep breath, he held the phone to his ear. "Mabel, I'm calling the Reverend Angus Willingham, over in—"

"Shucks, Preacher, no need to tell me where he lives, but he's been put in the County old folks home and they won't let the patients go to the phone, even if they're able, and I understand he ain't."

His heart wrenched. "Thank you, Mabel."

He hurried outside and rode ten miles, praying all the while that he wasn't too late. The home was once a hospital, before the county built a new one. Walking down the hall, the strong smell of antiseptic took his breath. A woman was on her hands and knees, scrubbing the floor.

"Ma'am do you know if Brother Angus Willingham is . . . in here?" His knees knocked as he waited for her answer.

She reached up and with the back of her hand, wiped the hair from her eyes. She pointed down the hall. "Room 12."

"Thank you!" He rushed down, then halted in front of the door. Would he be prepared to see his dear old friend, incapacitated? Guilt overwhelmed him. Why had he waited so long? Blowing out a breath of air, he gently knocked.

A feeble voice answered. "Please, come in."

A sense of relief surged when Cass saw the old fellow sitting up in bed with his signature smile.

"Well, blow me down! Come on in, son. I'm so glad you came. I had you on my mind this morning and said a little prayer for you. How are things going?"

"Not so good, Brother Angus. And you?"

"I'm doing great, just waiting for the call."

"The call, sir?"

"Yeah. For the Lord to call me home. It's closer than it's ever been and Praise God, before long I'll be walking those streets of gold with my Jesus. I got a heap of friends and kinfolks up there that I'm eager to see. In fact, I have more on that side than I do on this one. But enough about me. I got a feeling you got something weighin' on your mind. What's going on?"

Cass poured out his heart, sharing all about Rebekah. Then, he reached in his pocket and took out Amelia's letter detailing the fake drowning and her request for a divorce.

"So, what is it you're asking of me, Cass?"

He rubbed the back of his neck. "I suppose I came here seeking confirmation that I'd be justified in signing the papers."

"Son, you came to the wrong source. I'm not the one who

justifies. Is a divorce what you want?"

"To be honest, when I finished reading her letter, I was so angry, disgusted, and hurt, it immediately became what I wanted, too, but if I sign the papers, will I be just as guilty as Amelia?"

"Cass, this is something between you and God."

Why was the old man was giving him the run-around? He'd always known him to be very direct. "Amelia's made it clear that she wants no part of me or the children. She's living with another man. How can I be expected to take her back? She left my bed long before she left me." He clutched his hat in his hand. "I came here because I have faith that you'll tell me what I should do."

"Cass, your faith is ill-placed. What matters is what God is telling you. Go home, pray and search the scriptures until you have a peace that your direction is coming from above and not from the opinion of an old man. God's word provides assurance. Opinions leave you vulnerable to doubts, which the devil will cunningly use to crush you and steal your peace."

He knew the old man was right. How many times had he preached it, himself?

A nurse came in. "Sir, you'll have to leave now. It's time for Reverend Willingham's bath."

He nodded. "Thanks, Brother Angus. I promise not to wait so long to come back." Cass went directly from the old folks' home to his stump. Sitting there with his Bible, he searched the scriptures. The verse he had quoted so many times pierced his heart, "What God hath joined together, let no man put asunder." He'd only known two couples during his entire ministry to divorce and it wasn't a subject he'd given much thought to. Just before closing his Bible, his eyes fell on a verse, Matthew 19:9. He had his answer.

He closed his Bible and went home.

Sitting at his desk, he pulled out a pen and dipped it in the ink well. Reading the words on the document once more, he put the pen to the paper and signed his name. Not wanting to mail it from Vinegar Bend, where Albert, the Postmaster could question why he'd be sending mail to a Riverboat Casino in New Orleans, he pulled his satchel from the closet and placed the envelope inside. He'd mail it from the Post Office in McIntosh.

The words he sang on the way home from the stump came to mind and gave him an idea for his next lecture. Sure, he was hurt and felt betrayed. But God's grace had brought him through the pain of hearing that his children's mother had drowned, and by the grace of God he'd get through the pain and stigma of being a divorced preacher.

"Down in the human heart, crushed by the tempter, Feelings lie buried that only grace can restore."

He'd draw that ol' serpent, Satan, shooting arrows at the human heart and preach his next sermon on God's amazing grace.

Satan aims for the heart

CHAPTER 9

Saturday morning, Cass woke Gazelle at dawn. "Hon, something has come up. I need to run an errand and I'd like you to watch the younger ones while I'm gone. After you fix breakfast, tell Goat to cut a mess of turnip greens, and you'll find a slab of salt pork in the ice box to cook for dinner. I should be back mid-afternoon."

Her bottom lip poked out. "I have to do everything. Cook breakfast, Gazelle. Cook dinner, Gazelle. Cook supper, Gazelle. Watch the twins, Gazelle. Feed and change Gopher, Gazelle. It's not fair. All Goat has to do is cut a few greens."

Cass wasn't sure where the rage inside him came from. He never shouted at the children, but the words tumbled out before he could stop them. "I'm sick and tired of hearing you grumble about your responsibilities. We had help, but you made it impossible for her to stay here. Rebekah was the best thing that has happened to us in a very long time, yet you ran her off." He rubbed his hand across his eyes, then held out his arms to embrace her, but she instinctively pulled away.

"Sweetheart, I'm sorry. I'm so sorry. I don't know what got into me. It wasn't your fault she left. I never should've said that."

Tears welled in her eyes. "But you did say it and I know why."

His brow furrowed. "Oh?"

"You were in love with her, weren't you? I could see it every time you looked at her. You never looked at Mother with that same look in your eye. And you call yourself a man of God. Well, I suppose when David looked at Bathsheba with that same gleam, he too, considered himself to be a man of God."

Cass's instinct was to lash out at her for making such a crude remark, certainly unbefitting a young lady. But was she wrong? Was it so obvious that a twelve-year-old could see the longing in his eyes? He suddenly felt unclean—unworthy to preach about the wiles of the devil after he'd allowed the evil one access into his deepest thoughts. Allowed access? Who was he kidding? He'd invited him in and encouraged him to linger.

It pained him to think of his sweet Gazelle, who had always felt he could do no harm, to see through his shameful facade. Feeling defenseless, he walked out the door with his satchel in his hand.

Halfway between the house and McIntosh, the clouds opened, and the drenching rain made the dirt road virtually impassable. Cass pulled the buggy up in front of Maude's Café in downtown Vinegar Bend and decided to wait until the downpour slackened.

Rebekah sat near the window in the Café, when she looked out and spotted Cass driving up in his buggy. She slumped down in her chair and turned her head toward the wall, hoping he wouldn't spot her. Wanting to sneak out the back door, she would have, if Maude hadn't walked up with the oatmeal she ordered, just prior to Cass's unexpected entrance.

"Thank you," she whispered. With her head lowered, she watched out the corner of her eye as Cass took a seat on the opposite side of the room.

Maude yelled from behind the cash register. "'Morning, preacher. I thought you'd be down about Fruitdale. Isn't it their week?"

Rebekah couldn't hear his answer, but Maude was correct—it was his week to be in Fruitdale. It stood to reason he stopped in to avoid driving the buggy in the thunderous rain. But she was still puzzled why a man as wealthy as Cass would be driving a one-horse buggy when he obviously could afford a motor vehicle. However, there were a lot of things about Cass Marlowe that puzzled her.

She became fidgety when he seemed to linger, long after finishing his breakfast. If only he'd leave, so she could get to work, but the rain showed no signs of letting up. Even though the Millinery was only a few doors down, she should've been there ten minutes ago. How could she ever explain to Miss Elsie why she was late?

When a young fellow walked into the café and headed over to

Cass's table, she took it as the perfect opportunity to pay and get out, while he was occupied. She paid for her oatmeal and coffee, and quietly headed toward the door, when Maude yelled, "Sugar, you dropped your handkerchief."

Every head in the café turned in her direction. Every head, including Cass Marlowe's. Rebekah's heart hammered. She turned and looked near the register and spotted her handkerchief on the plank floor. Just as she reached down to pick it up, her head almost collided with Cass's. He stood, handkerchief in his hand, and held it out to her.

He said, "Fancy meeting you here."

Was he angry that she took his money for a ticket to Sipsey Ridge, yet remained in Vinegar Bend? She glanced from side-to-side to see if anyone was in hearing distance, then whispered. "I can explain."

"You owe me no explanation."

"Cass, I'll pay you back for the ticket. I promise. I have me a job. It doesn't pay a lot, but then I don't require much."

"Rebekah, you owe me nothing. I sent for you to come, and it was only right that I should pay for you to leave, when it became apparent things weren't working out as I had hoped. Where you choose to live or work is of no concern of mine."

His words cut to the bone, though she couldn't imagine why. Did she honestly fool herself into believing anything she said or anywhere she went could possibly be of concern to Cass Marlowe?

Rebekah was surprised how fast the days flew by and how long the nights were, as she lay awake thinking of the Marlowe children. Sure, Gazelle was hard to get along with, but didn't the child have a right to be angry? The responsibility was too much for a twelve-year-old to undertake alone—especially a child born in luxury, who had never had to shoulder any responsibility. Then, almost overnight she'd lost her mother and her Aunt Jewel. From listening to the children speak of their aunt, Rebekah concluded that the elderly woman had been the glue that held the family together. Not only had she been the cook and housekeeper, but nursemaid and chief caretaker.

Rebekah swallowed hard. How desperate Cass must have felt to have agreed to marry her, sight unseen, for the sake of the children. Why didn't she try harder?

The haunting regrets were put to rest during the daylight hours, when she became too busy to dwell on it. Miss Elsie taught her to make hats and called her a natural. The end of her first week, her boss lady brought out two lovely dresses and insisted Rebekah try them on.

"Oh, Miz Elsie, they're beautiful, but can I really afford them?"

"Please dear, call me Elsie. Not Miz Elsie. And I can't afford for you not to have them."

"I don't understand."

"You can't continue wearing the same dress day after day. I made these two for myself, but I've put on weight and can no longer wear them. I can't sell used merchandise, so I'd like for you to model them. It will be good for business."

Rebekah quickly concluded she'd never met anyone so kind as Elsie Drummond. Though her hair was beginning to gray and tiny wrinkles appeared around the corner of her eyes and mouth, she was still quite a looker. Rebekah had never been good at guessing one's age but surmised her boss lady was probably in her late thirties or early forties. She could only imagine how beautiful Elsie must've been, twenty years ago. What would cause such an attractive lady to wind up an old maid? Surely, she must've had plenty of beaus back in the day.

****

In a matter of weeks, Rebekah had more millinery orders than she could keep up with, yet she could never have chosen a line of work that would bring her so much satisfaction. Elsie even insisted that she wear her hat creations at work, since it brought in more business. The ladies in town took to her and loved having Rebekah sit them in front of the mirror to help them find the most becoming style hat for their shape face.

Rebekah passed by a full-length mirror and marveled at the image. Her hair was growing out nicely and now hung in loose ringlets over her shoulders. Dressed in one of her finest hats, a beautiful dress that fit her as if he were made for her, and the boots Cass gave her, she contrasted the image with the barefoot girl from No-Hope, with bobbed hair and wearing ill-fitting overalls.

****

Cass put Gopher to bed and called a family meeting. Goat sat on the opposite side of the divan from his father, Goose climbed up in her father's lap and Gander sprawled out on the floor in front of the fireplace. "Goat, where's your sister?"

Goat lifted the corner of his lip and pointed to Goose. "Raise your hand, sister."

Goose appeared to find her brother's cavalier attitude to be laughable. With one hand over her lips and the other waving in the air, she said, "Here I am, Father."

Cass attempted to stay calm, but lately it almost seemed as if the children deliberately tried to annoy him. "I think you both know I was referring to Gazelle."

Goat's shoulders lifted in sync with his brow. "I don't know where she is. Should I go find her?"

"Not yet. We'll wait a few minutes more." Cass let out a heavy breath when Gazelle ambled into the room and plopped down as far away as she could get from the family. Sometimes he wondered if he was too lenient with her but knowing how to handle a twelve-year-old girl who thought she was grown had become a daunting task.

"Now, that we're all here, I need to share something that will affect every member of this family. As you know, I married Rebekah because I felt I was placing too much responsibility on you and Goat. It wasn't right, yet it seemed to me at the time that my only option—other than taking a wife—would be to give up the ministry and stay home, and yet I didn't feel in my heart that was the way the Lord was leading."

Gazelle mumbled.

Cass stopped. "Would you mind speaking where we can all hear?"

"Never mind. No one cares what I think, anyway."

"I care, Gazelle."

"Then why did you marry Rebekah."

He placed a closed fist over his lips. Speaking slowly, he said, "Were you not listening? I believe I just explained my reasoning. As it turned out, the decision was a bad one."

"I agree we need someone to help when you're away, but not someone like her."

"What do you mean?"

"She wanted to boss me around and I'm not gonna take orders from someone who is only a few years older than me."

"I think you're wrong, Gazelle. Rebekah never tried to boss you, although I wouldn't have blamed her if she had. You were quite rude to her, but we can all agree that Rebekah didn't work out."

"Well, I don't know why you had to marry her. She was too young."

The room was quiet. Goose raised her hand. "I liked Rebekah. Why don't you go find her and tell her to come back but that she can't boss Gazelle."

Goat rolled his eyes. "She didn't boss her, Goose. If anything,

Gazelle bossed Rebekah. I liked her, too, but she wouldn't come back now, after the mean way Gazelle treated her, and I wouldn't blame her."

Gazelle opened her mouth, but Cass lifted his palm. "Hold it." He slid Goose from his lap and walked over and knelt beside Gazelle. "Honey, what was it about Rebekah that made you uncomfortable?"

"I told you already. She was too young."

"Was that your only complaint?"

She shrugged. "I guess." She turned her head. "Besides, she was—"

"Finish. She was what?"

"Well . . . pretty. I thought you liked her because of how she looked and not because you wanted someone to take care of us."

Goat cackled. "Why would he want to choose an ugly wife, Gazelle? That's crazy. If I was picking a wife, I'd want her to be easy to look at."

Cass frowned. "Goat, please allow me to finish the conversation with Gazelle. "So, if I should find an older lady who would agree to marry us, would you still be upset?"

"I'm not saying she has to be as old as Aunt Jewel. I just think you should marry someone your own age."

Cass opened his mouth to speak, then slowly shaking his head, decided it best to drop it.

Goat stood. "So, the meeting is over, right? Now, I'd like to finish playing baseball with the fellows in the pasture. May I be excused?"

Cass nodded. Gazelle had made her wants known. She preferred an older, homely looking woman. Not that it mattered to him, but Gazelle might soon discover she would've been much better off with someone near her age, rather than with someone who would feel it her matronly duty to keep a strong-willed twelve-year-old in line.

CHAPTER 10

The dress shop was taking more orders than Elsie had ever dreamed possible.

Women from neighboring towns were all talking about Rebekah's hats and though her commission soon doubled, for convenience sake, she chose to remain living in the upstairs room. On the nights she found it impossible to sleep, she could go downstairs and work on her hats. The only thing she missed having was a kitchen, but Maude opened at five o'clock every morning and closed at night whenever the notion struck her.

Rebekah was sitting in the cafe after work, drinking coffee and looking through the daily paper, when her gaze fixed on an ad for a wife. A sarcastic chortle escaped her lips. *Good luck with that.* Though she flipped the page, her thoughts lingered on the want-ad, and her curiosity led her to turn back. Not that she was interested in answering such a plea. Not interested at all. Her eyes skimmed the Classifieds, until she found it again:

Wife Wanted.
Widower with five young children.
Must be clean, of good character
Love children, Not afraid of hard work.
Reply to Box #213,
Fruitdale, Alabama.

Her throat constricted. *Cass.* It had to be. How many widowers with five children would be looking for a wife? Though the address listed Fruitdale, Rebekah was certain he gave the location of one of the schools where he lectured. No doubt, he chose not to get a Post Office box in Vinegar Bend, in order to protect his identity.

"Hey, mind if I join you for supper?"

Rebekah recognized Elsie's voice, even before looking up. Quickly laying the paper aside, she said, "Sure. Have a seat. I thought you went home."

"I didn't feel like cooking tonight and since Maude cooks corned beef and cabbage on Thursdays, I thought I'd come indulge myself. What did you order?"

"I haven't ordered, but that sounds good. I just sat down and picked up the paper."

"Anything newsworthy?"

Rebekah smiled. "Not that I've seen."

"Mind if I take a look?"

Rebekah picked up the paper and slid it across the table.

Maude yelled. "What are you ladies having?"

Elsie said, "Bring us your special." She thumbed through the pages to the Classifieds. She popped her hand over her mouth. "Oh, dear. Oh, dear me. How terribly sad."

"What's wrong? Did someone die?"

She shook her head. "No. I'm sorry. I just happened to see an ad in the paper for a mail-order bride."

Rebekah's hand shook when she picked up her coffee cup. She took a sip, then blotted her lips with a napkin. Her voice quaked. "Uh . . . someone you know?"

Elsie laid the paper aside. "What, dear?"

"I asked if you knew him?"

"Him?"

"Yes, the man looking for a wife."

"Oh, no. He's from Fruitdale and the only person I know from there is a distant cousin, but it doesn't prevent me from feeling pity. I'm sure it isn't easy for a man to hold a job and raise a houseful of children by himself."

Rebekah nodded. "I'm sure you're right. But what about you, Elsie? Have you ever considered responding to one of these ads for a Mail-Order Bride? I don't mean one like this, of course, where the man has a ready-made family."

"Me? Of course not." She picked up her water glass. "Why? Have you?"

Rebekah felt her face flush. "No."

After Maude brought out their meal, they ate in silence. Elsie said, "You seem a bit troubled tonight. Anything you'd like to talk about?"

"Not really." Rebekah paused, then added, "Well, I have no right to ask, since it's none of my business."

Elsie laid down her fork. "Honey, you should know by now, you can ask me anything. If I feel it's none of your business, I'll have no problem saying so. Now, what's on your mind?"

"Elsie, you are an attractive woman and I'm sure you were a real beauty in your day. Why did you choose not to marry?" Rebekah's stomach knotted, seeing the hurtful look in Elsie's eyes. Embarrassed that she'd been so nosey, she quickly blurted, "I'm sorry. That was rude of me to ask. I didn't mean to offend you."

Elsie gave a faint smile. "I'll admit, your question took me aback, but I'm not offended. I'm sure many people in Vinegar Bend have wondered the same thing, and it's not been for a lack of proposals. I've courted several prominent men in the past fourteen years, but there has only been one man for me."

"How sad. What happened? Did he die?"

Her lip quivered. "I think death would've been less painful. But, alas, a wicked, conniving woman won his heart. Since then, I've not found anyone who could fill his shoes. I'm sure you couldn't possibly understand what I'm saying, although I was about your age when I fell in love."

Maude walked over. "Ladies, I hate to shoo you out, but I see you've finished your meal, and I'm ready to get home. It's been a long day."

Elsie said, "My goodness, I didn't realize how long we'd been sitting here. My apologies. Rebekah and I are together all day, and there was no need for us to linger any longer. The corned beef was delicious, as always."

Rebekah picked up her purse from the adjoining chair and pulled out the correct change. "Goodnight Maude. And goodnight, Elsie. See you in the morning."

She walked back to the dress shop and trudged up the stairs. Tossing and turning in bed, the night seemed even longer than usual. Would she wind up like Elsie—alone and childless, with no one to be waiting for her at the end of the day? She knew the answer. No man could ever make her heart flutter the way it fluttered when Cass looked at her. So, he didn't love her. She could've been satisfied loving him for the rest of her life, but she'd destroyed all hope. Now, that she'd seen the best, no other man could ever measure up. Elsie was wrong—Rebekah understood perfectly.

****

Cass couldn't sleep at night. Whatever possessed him to do such an idiotic thing? Maybe it wasn't too late to cancel the ad. Monday morning, he called the Fruitdale local newspaper and asked to speak to the Editor.

"Sir, I recently mailed in an advertisement to be printed in your newspaper, along with seventy-five cents to cover printing, but I have since changed my mind and would like to withdraw the ad."

"I see. So, I suppose you're wanting a refund?"

"No sir. I simply don't wish for it to be printed."

"What was the advertisement for?"

Cass swallowed hard. "Wife Wanted." Hearing a chuckle, he stiffened.

"I'll look it up to see if it's already gone to press. Hold on while I check."

The seconds seemed like minutes, as Cass waited.

Just as he was about to hang up, the editor said, "Well, well, I think I found it: Lonely Bachelor Seeking Companionship. Correct?"

Cass bit his lip. "No. That's not it."

"Sorry. What's the name on the envelope? Perhaps it's still on the desk."

Cass stuttered. "I . . I didn't give my name. The box number is 213."

"I hate to tell you, Mr. Two-Thirteen, but I'm afraid it's too late. But I don't think you have anything to worry about. I can't imagine you'll have to check your box for replies. I mean, how many women would you think would be seeking to marry a man with five young'uns?" He laughed again, this time louder. "You could've omitted the line, 'Not afraid of hard work.' After all, if any woman is fool enough to respond to such an ad, you can bet she's not afraid of hard work."

"So, you're saying it has already gone to press?"

"I'm saying if you'll check your morning paper, you'll find it on page four, third column."

"Thank you, sir." He hung up the phone and buried his face in his hands. What had he done? Attempting to calm his nerves, he tried to believe the editor was correct and there'd be no responses. He closed his eyes and prayed. "Lord, you promise that all things will work together for good to those who love you and are called according to your purpose, but I'm finding my faith wavering." His voice cracked with emotion. "I do love you, Father, and I believe with all my heart you've called me into this ministry. You've gifted me with a unique talent to illustrate Bible lectures on the chalkboard. I have felt you hand-picked the communities on the circuit, where you desire that I go. But I have five children. How can I be in two places at one time? Please, God, tell me how in my situation that all things will work according to my good?"

Gazelle walked in the room and seeing her father in prayer, mumbled. "Sorry."

Cass lifted his head and feigned a smile. "Come on in, sweetheart. What can I help you with?"

She ran over and threw her arms around his neck. "Father, I'm sorry that I didn't try harder with Rebekah. To tell the truth, I was jealous. She was prettier than me and I was afraid you'd love her more than you love me."

Cass hugged his daughter and stroked a strand of hair from her face. "Oh, punkin, no one could ever take your place with me. No one. How could you even think such?"

"I don't know, but I did." She walked over and sat in the high-back rocker. "If you know where she went, beg her to come back and tell her I'm sorry I caused her to leave."

"No, Gazelle. I've told you it wasn't your fault. Rebekah left because she wasn't mature enough to handle the situation. It had nothing to do with you. But after countless hours of trying to figure out how to balance riding the circuit with raising my family, I'm thinking my place is here with you children."

"Give up the ministry? Oh, Father, you can't do that. We can put an ad in the newspaper for a housekeeper. I'm sure there are women who are having a difficult time making ends meet. I'd think they'd be grateful for the job."

"Hon, if we could manage with a housekeeper to care for Gopher during the day, that might be fine. But we need a woman who not only is here for him during the day after you children go back to school, but who'll be here at night to walk the floor with him when he's in pain. I thought his colic would end after the first three months, but you understand as well as I, how many times he wakes up screaming at night."

Her chin trembled. "Then I'll quit school to be here during the day, and if I'm not going to school, I can continue to get up with him at night."

"No, baby. I won't hear of you dropping out of school. That's not an option. I've been depending on you more than I should have since Aunt Jewel died and it isn't right."

"I know I've complained a lot, Father, but I promise to do better. I don't want you to give up the ministry. I know how much it means to you."

"Honey, trust me, I've languished over this for hours on end, but I'm afraid there's no other way. Gopher needs stability. When he wakes up in pain, it's imperative that he see the same face—the same arms reaching out to him, offering comfort. The same lap cuddling him, as he rocks off to sleep. Not a different nursemaid every couple of weeks and that would be a likely scenario. He's not the easiest baby to care for."

She giggled. "You can say that again. He's a little terror. Were we that much trouble?"

Cass shook his head. "No. You were a very good baby. You woke up for a two o'clock feeding and would fall back to sleep. It took a little longer for Goat to get into a schedule, but he soon came around. The twins were happy babies but required more attention, simply because there were two of them." His gaze shifted to the floor. "And then there's colicky little Gopher, who requires more attention than all four of you put together."

Gazelle's eyes darkened. "Yessir, I can believe that." She wrung her hands. "Father, I haven't wanted to ask, since I was hoping you'd bring it up first, but I think it's time we admitted the truth."

"The truth? Punkin, you know there's nothing you can't talk to me about. What's on your mind?"

"Gopher *is* different . . . and I think we're kidding ourselves to keep blaming it on colic. I know you see it, too."

CHAPTER 11

Cass felt as if someone had socked him in the stomach. He sucked in a lungful of air and let it out slowly, as he attempted to gather his thoughts. It wasn't as if the crazy notion hadn't tried to creep into his mind. He understood where Gazelle was coming from, but she was wrong. Gopher was a normal baby . . . a normal baby with a prolonged case of colic. It had been impossible not to feel sorry for him and to spoil him in the process.

Seeing Gazelle waiting for his answer, he feigned a smile. "You want to know what's wrong with your little brother? Spoiled. I'm afraid we've spoiled him." Cass wanted to believe the words coming from his lips. But was that really all there was to it? Doc Brunson had prescribed Paregoric months ago to ease the pain. It was a temporary fix and would put him to sleep. And even though the doctor didn't appear alarmed, Cass had begun to worry about the effects such strong medication might have on his little Gopher.

Whether Gazelle believed it or not, she didn't pursue it.

"Father, Gopher needs special care and I can't let you give up the ministry. Mother would not have wanted it, either."

Gazelle was right. Amelia wouldn't have wanted it. He recalled how she encouraged him to spend time on the circuit. Until the letter came, he'd felt blessed to have a wife who was not jealous of the hours he spent away. She even encouraged him to seek out new venues. Never once did he suspect her motives, yet now his thoughts were bombarded with haunting questions. There was one that troubled him more than all the others, yet he'd never have an answer. Was she unfaithful before she left? Wouldn't knowing the truth be easier than wondering for the rest of his life? Or would it? Looking back, he could remember Aunt Jewel making remarks that had no meaning at the time. Now, they were beginning to make sense.

The frightening thought was interrupted when Gazelle said, "Father, either I quit school, or we find a nice lady to help us. Your chalkboard lectures have changed many lives. God has equipped you for this ministry. Could you honestly give it up?"

"Gazelle, it's not what I want, but even if I were open to the idea of hiring a live-in housekeeper, I don't envision one staying longer than a couple of nights, and I think that would lead to Gopher having even bigger problems."

"You don't know that. So why don't we put an ad in the paper for someone who doesn't look at this as a temporary job."

"You make it sound easy, sweetheart. If only it were that

simple."

"It could be."

"Honey, I know it's hard for you to understand, but it's not fitting for a widowed man of my reputation to employ a live-in housekeeper unless, of course she's of the age no one would have cause to gossip. But alas, the responsibility of taking care of this household would be asking too much of an elderly woman. Trust me, I've given much thought to the matter, but our situation is quite complicated."

"Father, you have a lot to offer any woman. Forget housekeeper. I think you should advertise for a wife."

He chuckled. Not a ha-ha sort of chuckle, but a nervous-sounding chortle. "Funny, you should say that, darling. As a matter of fact, I did put an ad in the paper."

"You mean it?"

"Yes, but I realize now, I shouldn't have been in such a hurry. I don't want to marry a woman who feels it her 'job' to care for you and your siblings."

"I'm confused. I thought that's what you did want."

"It was."

"Then I don't understand."

"It shouldn't be about what I want, but what God wants for our family. I have a lecture centered on the scripture that says, 'Wait on the Lord. Wait, I say.' In my lecture, I draw a picture of a lonely-looking man, who spends hours on his knees pleading with God for a helpmate. But instead of waiting on the Lord, he gives place to the evil one, and soon he's no longer on his knees, but sitting on the fence, all the while talking to God, but giving an ear to the devil. Listening to the wrong voice, he begins to frequent the bars, searching for a woman who can fill the loneliness in his heart. The lust of the eyes tempts him and he marries a woman of ill repute, believing he'll change her. Instead, she changes him and he lives out a life of misery. If only he'd waited on the Lord instead of getting ahead of him, he could've lived a long and fulfilling life.

Honey, don't you see? The Lord has a plan for each of us, but too often, we grow weary in the wait and thus become hasty and take matters into our own hands, instead of waiting on God. Perhaps it's time I start practicing what I preach."

Gazelle's shoulders lifted. "I don't get it. How do you know it wasn't God leading you to place the ad?"

How could he make her understand, when he wasn't sure he understood, himself? Reaching over and placing his hand on her shoulder, he said, "Honey, I won't deny that I sometimes get confused and miss God but it happens when I get in a hurry for an answer."

"Father, I believe God led you to send in the ad, but you've climbed up on that fence. Satan wants to confuse you into thinking you were wrong. Didn't you tell me that confusion is of the devil?"

His gaze locked with his daughter's. She was growing up so fast. When did she get so wise? Could she be right? "Gazelle, I want to be careful that I don't make the same mistake I made by marrying Rebekah. I was too hasty in my decision. If I'd only waited on the Lord, it would've saved all of us—Rebekah included—from going through such a trying experience. I'm tired of striving. I'm beginning to believe that if God has truly called me into the ministry—and I have reason to fully believe that He has—then He'll supply my every need. That includes a woman who will love all five of you, just as I do."

When his mind wandered, he failed to hear Gazelle's response. If their own mother found it too large a task, how could he possibly expect a stranger to care more?

"Father? What do you think of my idea?"

"I'm sorry, sweetheart. What idea?"

"You continue the ministry God has given you, and I'll answer those who respond to the want-ad." She lowered her head and giggled. "Don't worry. I won't rule out anyone just because she happens to be attractive."

Cass smiled. "Honey, it's not the outward appearance but what's in the heart that matters."

"Are you saying you'll allow me to screen the applicants?"

Obviously, she misinterpreted his words, but she seemed enthused and what would it hurt to grant her permission? He recalled the newspaper editor's comment and completely agreed. What woman in her right mind *would* respond when there were six other ads from single bachelors seeking wives? His lip curled. Besides, even if the perfect woman replied, what good would it do to commit to a marriage agreement if his high-strung little Gazelle didn't approve.

"Gazelle, I want you to understand, like the man in my lecture, I was hasty in submitting the ad. I'm not expecting any responses. However, if there should be one, it would first go to a box number in Fruitdale. But I filled out a form at the same time I sent in the ad, for all correspondence addressed to my box in Fruitdale to be redirected to our home address."

She giggled. "Why would you do that?" Not waiting for an answer, she said, "Oh, I get it. You didn't want Mr. Thornton at the Post Office in Vinegar Bend to question why you'd be mailing a letter to the newspaper."

Cass winked. "You do understand your Father, sweetpea."

Suddenly sounding much older than her years, she said, "Then it's settled. Tomorrow is Tuesday. I'll have you packed and your breakfast ready at daybreak. I'll expect you back Friday, and we'll hope I have good news upon your return. It's important to me to prove to you I can handle this. I really want you to go."

"Sugar, are you sure about this? I don't feel right leaving you with so much responsibility. What if Gopher should get sick."

"I would send Goat to fetch the doc. Now, stop worrying. You have a job to do. If we're fortunate, this will be your last trip on the circuit before I find the perfect helpmate for you."

Maybe she was right. Perhaps this was the answer he prayed for. Though she was only twelve, Gazelle had always had a good head on her shoulders. A scripture came to mind, reinforcing his decision. The fields were white ready for harvest. He'd sensed the beginning of a revival in McIntosh on his last trip. Now was not the time to walk away.

****

Gazelle walked her father to the buggy at the crack of dawn. "Now, don't you worry about a thing. Everything is under control. There's plenty of food in the icebox, Gopher hasn't had any sick spells in two nights—and who knows? Maybe he's outgrowing them. But if not, I know what to do.

When the children wake up, I'll tell Goat to hitch up the mule and ride over to the Glovers' to pick up butter and eggs, to make sure we have enough to last through the weekend. There's money in the sugar jar. It should be plenty until you return.

Cass bit his lip as he held his daughter in a tight squeeze. Was he doing the right thing by leaving her with so much responsibility?

She pulled away, then placed both hands on his back and playfully pushed.

"Honey, if you should need me—"

"Would you please go? We'll be fine."

He climbed up in the buggy. "Oh, I almost forgot. Tell Goat I said to take Gander fishing but be patient with him. Goose will probably pitch a fit to go but tell her I'll take her as soon as I can. Goat doesn't need to have them both down at the river."

Shaking her head, she giggled. "Bye, Father. Please trust me."

He returned her wave and rode off, yet he was certain there was something he forgot.

103

The trip was long, giving him more time to spend talking with the Lord without all the interruptions. How could he have been so fooled by Amelia? Gazelle thought her mother could do no wrong. He could never allow her to know the truth. Was Gopher's problems related to a mother who resented him from the inception? Cass recalled a disturbing conversation, shortly after the baby was born. As shocking as it was when Amelia flung open her robe and screamed, "Look at me—it's disgusting what those kids have done to me."

When he failed to understand what she meant, she flung a vase at him and shouted.

"No woman had a better figure than I, and now I look like ol' lady Bloodworth."

Gopher was barely two weeks old at the time, and Cass recalled trying to assure her she was still beautiful, yet the harder he tried to convince her, the angrier she became.

She'd never had trouble regaining her figure, even after the birth of the twins. When he confided in Aunt Jewel, she assured him it was quite normal for a woman to go through a bout of depression following childbirth, and there was no need for alarm. All would be back to normal in a matter of time. He wanted to believe it was true, though Amelia had completely shut him out— not only out of the bedroom, but out of her life.

Taking Aunt Jewel's advice, he tried to be patient, though it became increasingly difficult to overlook the effect Amelia's sporadic tirades were having on the children. Looking back, he realized things between them hadn't been right, long before Gopher's birth, though he'd been in denial. He was a preacher, for goodness sake. He was supposed to know how to be a good husband, yet apparently, he was a failure.

His throat tightened, recalling the most painful day of his life. Five weeks and three days after Gopher was born, he was in the middle of a chalkboard lecture when a telegram came, saying his wife was presumed drowned.

Reliving the horrifying memory brought on a feeling of intense nausea. He pulled the buggy over to the side of the road, leaned over and heaved until his stomach ached. With no one around to hear his plea, he looked up into the heavens and shouted, "What am I to do, Lord? Tell me, please. What am I supposed to do? When I travel the circuit, I feel I'm neglecting my children. Yet, when I stay home with them, I feel I'm neglecting what you've called me to do. How can I possibly balance both?"

****

Elsie was too excited to go to bed. In the past year, she'd taken more pies and fried chicken over to Cass than she could keep count of, yet not once had he invited her into his home. She'd begun to think he wanted her to leave him alone, but after seeing the advertisement in the classifieds, her thinking changed. She could only imagine the poor man was overwhelmed with responsibility and had too much pride to admit he'd been wrong when he chose Amelia over her. Elsie couldn't remember being this happy in a very long time.

When the cat nuzzled her legs, she reached down and held him to her breast and stroked his fur. "Don't you see what this means, Packy? Cass sent me a message. He knew I'd see the ad and recognize it as coming from him, but he has too much pride to admit he made a mistake." The cat wriggled out of her arms and sailed across the room.

Elsie stood in front of the closet debating on what to wear to his house. It was then she remembered the red dress with a white pinafore packed in her hope chest. Opening the chest, it was just as beautiful as she remembered when she packed it, hoping to wear it on her Honeymoon, fourteen years ago. Elsie shook it, allowing any wrinkles to fall out, then walked over to the mirror and held it in front of her. Perfect. People had often told her red was her color. "What do you think, Packy?" Laughing out loud when the cat stood motionless, staring at the brilliant red color, she said, "I agree. It's gorgeous. I want his eyes to pop out when he sees me standing in his doorway." She picked up the cat. "Great idea. I'll do it. I'll close the shop a couple of hours early. Maybe Cass and I will take a stroll in the woods back of Amelia House, before sundown." Her throat tightened. The first thing she'd do after she and Cass married would be to change the name of Amelia House. It pained her every time she heard anyone call the mansion sitting atop the hill, Amelia House. But would Cass agree? After all, she was the mother of his children. Perhaps, she shouldn't suggest it too soon. Still, it didn't keep her from thinking of other appropriate names. Folks from all around would go there to view the rose garden. Why not call it Rose Hill? Or what about the gorgeous azaleas that bloomed in abandon every spring? It wouldn't be such a stretch to call it Azalea House. The cat jumped from her arms. "You're right, Packy. I like Rose Hill, much better."

When Packy scratched on the screen, Elsie walked into the kitchen and let him out through the back door, then dressed for bed. Her heart raced as she imagined what it would be like when Cass opened the door to see her standing there. After indulging herself in numerous romantic fantasies, she abandoned the idea of showing up unannounced, concluding it would be best to answer the ad, rather than risk the chance of him being surrounded by curious children when she arrived.

Pulling out a pen and paper, she wrote:

Dear Sir:

She stopped and giggled, imagining Cass laughing when he recognized her handwriting.

   This is in answer to your advertisement in the newspaper. I shall attempt to tell you about myself and hope . . . she wadded up the stationery and started over.

Dear Sir:

This is in answer to your plea in the newspaper. I am the one you are looking for. The wife who will love you with all my heart and will strive for the remainder of my life to make you happy. I'm in my mid-thirties and have never been married. I was in love fourteen years ago, but another woman wormed her way into the love of my life and broke my heart. However, being a real romantic, I'm ready to put the past behind me and start afresh. I'm told that I'm quite beautiful and look years younger than my age. I own a very successful shop. I only mention that, so you'll understand I'm not a gold-digger, and capable of supporting myself quite well.

I'll be eagerly awaiting your reply with a suggestion where you'd like to meet.

Sincerely Yours,

Your Lady-in-Waiting

Positive that the notice was meant for her to see, she read over her response to make sure she had provided enough information to identify herself, in the event he received other replies. She read it again. *Mid-thirties, beautiful, never married, although in love fourteen years ago, another woman causing breakup, and shop owner.* He couldn't miss it. Though she would have preferred him approaching her face-to-face, she supposed after their last confrontation, he was too proud to admit he'd been wrong. Besides, she found the subtlety to be quite romantic. It reminded her of unmasking at a masquerade party. Carefully folding the stationary, she tucked it inside an envelope, turned out the light, and lay awake imagining what it would be like, married to the only man she'd ever loved—the man she had continued to love for over fourteen long, lonely years.

CHAPTER 12

Gazelle awoke the following morning, filled with anticipation. She could hardly get her chores done for watching the mailbox. But alas, her heart fell when the postman rode past without stopping. Her father was right. It was irrational to think any woman would be looking for a man with five children.

There was only one thing to do. She had to insist that her father allow her to quit school. Even if a woman was foolish enough to answer the ad, it would take only one night with Gopher to make her pack up and leave. It was then her father's lecture of the man who gave up too quickly, instead of waiting for the promise, flooded her thoughts. She wouldn't give up. Regardless of how hopeless it seemed, she was determined to wait. Ashamed that she'd spent more time complaining than praying, Gazelle trekked across the pasture to an old oak stump where she'd seen her father sit for hours in prayer. Sensing there was something holy at that very spot, she sat down and with her hands covering her face, the words in her heart flowed from her lips. When she stood, she sensed a feeling of anticipation—the kind of eagerness she experienced every Christmas Eve, when waiting to unwrap the presents under the tree. She could never guess what surprise lay beneath the wrappings, but it was always exactly what she wanted, even when she hadn't known beforehand that she wanted it. Was that how it would be? Was God waiting to give her exactly what she wanted, even though she hadn't known what to ask for?

Hearing Goose calling her name, Gazelle hurried toward the house. "What's wrong, Goose?"

Wiping her nose with her hand, she sobbed, "Go . . . go . . . go—"

"Spit it out. Where do you want me to go?"

"No. I'm trying to tell you that Go . . . Gopher woke up. I tried to pick him up from the crib, but I dropped him and now he's screaming, and his nose is bleeding. I'm sorry, Gazelle. Goat washed the blood off, but he told me to come find you."

Gazelle wrapped her arm around her little sister. "It's okay, Goose. You wanted to help, but from now on, come get me or Goat to get him from his crib. Gopher's too heavy for you to lift."

"You aren't angry at me?" She wiped her eyes with the tail of her dress. "His nose is bleeding."

"No, I'm not angry, and he has nosebleeds all along." Gazelle wasn't sure which one of them was most surprised by her calm reaction. Anger had been a driving force in her life for a very long time.

****

Wednesday morning, Gazelle had Goat build a fire under the iron washpot. Although she'd never washed clothes before, she'd watched Aunt Jewel do it every Monday for as long as she could remember. After the elderly aunt died, her father had continued the Monday ritual. She'd prove to Father she was mature enough to handle things at home until God answered her prayer. While scrubbing one of Goat's shirts, she spotted the mailman and dropped both the shirt and scrub board into the scalding water and ran to meet him.

Shuffling through his mail pouch, he shouted, "Looks like someone gave out the wrong address for you folks. These letters all went to Fruitdale." Scratching his head, he mumbled, "Peculiar, indeed. Wonder how that happened."

Her heart hammered as she reached out for the envelopes. There was no doubt in her mind that God had indeed heard her prayer. From now on, she'd make a point to go to the stump anytime there was a pressing matter on her mind.

Gazelle ran past Goat. "Goat, would you please finish the wash? I have something very important to take care of."

"Me? That's a woman's work. You know I don't know how to wash clothes."

"Neither did I, but I managed to wash all but two shirts and they both happen to belong to you. So, if you want something to wear tomorrow, you might think about squeezing them out and getting them on the line." She didn't wait for a response but ran up the steps and didn't slow down until she reached her room.

She tore into the first envelope and read.

My dear sir,

I knead a job reel bad. My old man left me and the sorry old woman I worked fer fired me and said I stoll from her but she is a lier. I ain't never stoll nothing. When do you want to git married. Soon I hope.

Arnessa Butterworth
Irvington, Alabama

Gazelle's hopes were crushed. She wadded up the letter and tossed it in the trash can. Then opening the second envelope, she felt a sense of relief. The penmanship and spelling was much better.

To whom it may concern,

I recently saw your ad in the newspaper for a wife. I want you to understand I have never considered becoming a mail-order bride, but my husband has been dead for almost thirty years and I am tired of living alone. Henry and I didn't have children, but I have been a schoolteacher since I was sixteen and believe me, with my experience I know how to make even the toughest ones behave. There has never been an unruly child that I couldn't whip into line. I will look forward to hearing from you.

Yours truly,

Ida Maylene Roundtree.
Theodore, Alabama

"She must be old as Methuselah for her husband to have been dead thirty years." When Gopher cried, Gazelle tossed the letter in the trash basket with the other one and went to the kitchen to prepare Gopher's formula. She warmed the oatmeal she cooked the children for breakfast. It seemed futile to feed him when he always spat out more than he took in.

She picked up her little brother and plopped down in the rocker to feed him. Taking on the chores of a mother was a tougher job than she'd ever imagined. Why did God have to take Aunt Jewel when they needed her most?

Although finding her father a wife was a much harder job than she had anticipated, these past two days had convinced her that running a household was even harder. She couldn't afford to give up.

After she finished the dinner dishes and got the little ones down for their afternoon naps, she collapsed on the settee in the parlor, too tired to move. It was then that she remembered the one unopened envelope. With renewed energy Gazelle jumped up and ran up the stairs, skipping every other one. Trying not to get her hopes up, she held it in her hands and sucked in a deep breath before ripping it open.

Her eyes quickly skimmed over the contents.

"Dear Sir:

This is in answer to your plea in the newspaper. I am the one you are looking for."

Gazelle rolled her eyes, but the next sentence captured her attention.

"The wife who will love you with all my heart and will strive for the remainder of my life to make you happy. I'm in my mid-thirties and have never been married. I was in love fourteen years ago, but another woman wormed her way into the love of my life and broke my heart. However, being a real romantic, I'm ready to put the past behind me and start afresh. I'm told that I'm quite beautiful and look years younger than my age. I own a very successful shop. I only mention that, so you'll understand I'm not a gold-digger, and capable of supporting myself quite well.

I'll be eagerly awaiting your reply with a suggestion where you'd like to meet.

Sincerely Yours,

Your Lady-in-Waiting
P. O. Box 12
Vinegar Bend, Alabama

Gazelle squealed and flung her hand over her heart. "Perfect and she lives in Vinegar Bend."

Sitting down at her father's desk, she picked up a pen and dipped it in the inkwell. She wrote in her best hand.

Dear Lady-in-Waiting,

What a nice surprise it was to read your letter. Naturally, there are others who answered the ad, but it thrills me to tell you, yours was indeed the response I was waiting for. I would like to meet with you, Friday morning around ten o'clock at Maude's

Café. I feel it better to meet in there, to keep from having to explain your presence to the children. I hope Friday is convenient. I am most eager to see you.

Gazelle pondered how she should sign it. If she signed her own name, the woman might consider it a hoax and not show up. Yet, she dared not sign her father's name in case this woman wasn't as perfect as she appeared to be in the letter. Why sign it at all? She sealed it and while the twins were still asleep, she hitched up Patches and rode to town.

If she could get it to the Post Office by three o'clock, it would be placed in Mr. Miller's satchel to be delivered tomorrow. It was important that the interview take place Friday morning, Father would be returning in the evening, and she hoped to be able to surprise him with some very good news.

That evening when the phone rang, Goose raced to answer, but Gazelle grabbed it first. "Father, is that you?"

"Yes, sweetheart. How are things going at home?"

"Running like a well-oiled machine. Everything is hunky-dory."

He chuckled. "Wonderful. And Gopher?"

"Same as always, but we're managing fine." She paused. "Not that we couldn't use a little help around here, but I think that's about to happen real soon."

"Oh?"

She told him about the letters. "Two are hilarious. Shall I read them all to you?"

"Sure, but make it snappy, hon. This is long distance."

"Hold on." She ran across the room and picked up the letters from off the buffet, and after the second one, he said, "Perhaps we can save the last one until I get home on Friday."

"But you must hear this one, Father. I'll read fast," When she finished, she said, "The Lady-in-Waiting is the one who impressed me. What did you think?"

"If you were impressed, then I shall be, too. We need to hang up but tell the kids Father loves them and I miss you all very much. Bye, now."

"Bye, Father. See you Friday."

CHAPTER 13

Elsie awoke at 4:30 a.m. Friday morning with more energy than she'd had in years. Too early to leave for work, she mopped the linoleum rug in the bedroom and rearranged the furniture in the parlor. Rolling up the hook rug, she threw it over her shoulder, went outside and beat it on the clothesline by the light of the moon.

Though it seemed time was standing still, the sun finally peeked over the tops of the crepe myrtles, and Elsie gazed around, amazed at the chores she'd accomplished, which had been left undone far too long.

Her heart sank when the tiny covered buttons on the red dress lacked two inches reaching the buttonholes. No time to panic. She opened the bottom drawer to the armoire and pulled out a front-laced corset she'd worn only once and swore she'd never put herself through such torture again. But her heart was set on the red dress. Sucking in as far as she could, she stretched the horrid garment with all its bones, hooks and eyes as tight as she could pull it, then slid the dress over her head. After buttoning the last tiny button, she would've breathed a sigh of relief, if only she could breathe. Though it was still too early to go to work, she fed Packy and left, since there was nothing more to do at home.

Strolling down the street, she made a point to look at her reflection in every store window and she liked what she saw. Her heart raced like a giddy sixteen-year-old experiencing her first crush. But this was no crush. This was a love that had no end. When she reached Maude's, she spotted Rebekah sitting alone at a table.

Elsie thought she'd burst open with such great news bottled inside her, but wouldn't it be more appropriate to allow Cass to choose when and with whom to reveal the romantic details? After all, he had his children to consider. *The children.*

A queasy feeling in the pit of her stomach caused the taste of bile to rise to her throat. It wasn't that she didn't like kids. She did. Yet, she'd never known how to relate. Being an only child growing up with a Governess, her childhood was spent around adults. Would they like her—or resent her for taking their mother's place? Wishing to dismiss the negative thoughts, she whispered, "Mrs. Castle Marlowe," which brought a smile to her lips and made everything right again.

Rebekah shoved her chair back and sprang to her feet when Elsie walked in. "Well, this is a nice surprise. What are you doing in town so early?"

"It was such a beautiful morning, I thought it wicked to waste a single moment of this day."

Rebekah laughed. "Wicked?" Her eyes squinted as she gazed at her boss lady.

"Mind if I join you?"

"Please do and tell me what you have up that pretty sleeve of yours. I Suwannee, if you don't look like the cat that swallowed the mouse. What is it you aren't telling me, Elsie Drummond?"

Elsie snickered "Whatever do you mean? Would I keep something from my favorite milliner?"

"Yes, I think you would." Rebekah's gaze traveled from the top of Elsie's neatly coiffured hair and trailed slowly down to the lace at the bottom of the white pinafore. "I've never seen that dress. Is it new?"

Elsie reached her right hand to her left shoulder, fluffing out the puffed sleeve. "No, it isn't new, I've just been saving it for a special occasion. Do you like it?"

"It's gorgeous and red is a very becoming color on you. But what's so special about today?"

Elsie reached out and grasped Rebekah's hand. "Oh, honey, I wish I could tell you, but you'll know soon enough. Just be happy for me."

"Whatever it is, I *am* happy for you, Elsie. I don't know anyone who deserves happiness more than you. You're one of the sweetest, kindest persons I've ever known. You took me in when I had nowhere to go. You've taught me a trade and made me feel there's something I can do and do well. I'll always love you for changing my life for the better."

Elsie squeezed her hand. "It's I who owe you, my dear. My business has doubled in the short while you've been in my employ. And I have a strong hunch I will be relying on you even more in the future. I have a very important appointment before lunch today and I'm not sure if I can make it back before closing. Think you can handle the shop alone?"

"I'll do my best."

She reached over and laid her hand on top of Rebekah's. "I have no doubt you'll do just fine, dear. You're a very responsible young lady, and hiring you was one of the best decisions of my life."

Maude walked over to take their order, but Elsie waved her off. "Thanks, Maude, but I couldn't swallow a thing. A cup of coffee will be fine."

Maude's brows met in the middle. "Well, I can understand why you wouldn't be able to swallow. My goodness, you look like you're about to bust open in that dress."

Rebekah sensed the comment hadn't set well with Elsie, though she thought it best not to probe further. "I'll take the usual, Maude. A slice of cheese toast, if you please."

"I Suwannee, you eat like a bird, child. I don't reckon it's a bad thing, though. Chances are, you won't never have to bind yourself up like a mummy in one of them blasted corsets, the way some women do. But then, if I had your figure, I wouldn't want nothing to push or pull it no other way, but the way God put it all together."

Elsie cleared her throat. "That will be all, Maude. Coffee, please?"

Maude continued as if she hadn't heard. "I ain't never been built like you, sugar, even when I was young, but then I ain't never been ashamed to let it all hang out and if somebody don't like what they see, they can turn their head and look the other way. That's just how I feel."

Elsie's joy seemed to have been sapped. She'd hardly finished her coffee, when she stood and said, "Don't hurry, dear. You have plenty of time to enjoy your toast, but I think I'll be on my way. I'd like to rearrange the store window."

CHAPTER 14

Friday morning, Gazelle handed the baby to Goat and promised she'd bring home one of Maude's pound cakes if he'd watch the kids while she was gone.

He grumbled, "Don't stay any longer than need be. Gopher doesn't like me."

She laughed. "Gopher doesn't like anyone."

Hitching up the mule and wagon, she rode into town and arrived at the cafe thirty minutes early. A bell rang as the door opened. After glancing around inside, the muscles in her shoulders slowly relaxed, when she realized there was no one in the Cafe who would recognize her and pry into her business.

Maude yelled from the kitchen. "Have a seat anywhere. I'll be out there d'rectly."

Gazelle moseyed over to a table in the far corner of the room and sat down. She gnawed on her thumbnail. All the brilliant things she'd planned to say, suddenly escaped her. She'd never conducted an interview. What questions should she ask? Attempting to calm her fears, she concluded the woman had already answered the real important questions, else she wouldn't have been so eager to set up the meeting. This was simply a formality.

Maude came stomping out of the kitchen with two platters in her hand and plopped them down in front of a couple of strangers sitting near the door.

Turning toward Gazelle, her gold tooth sparkled when she grinned. Then, in a voice loud enough to be heard clear across the street she said, "Law, child, where did you come from? I haven't seen you in a month of Sundays . . .not since Jewel's funeral. How y'all doing, shug?"

"We're fine, thank you, Maude."

"Who's staying with you young'uns, now that Jewel's gone?"

"Uh, I am."

Maude tightened her lips and shook her head slowly. "And I 'spect you doing a good job, too. I wadn't much bigger than you, when I married Albert and took on the job of raising his six younger siblings. But what about when school starts back, sugar? Whatcha gonna do then?"

The bell on the door clanged and Maude didn't wait for her answer. She yelled, "Come on in. Elsie. What are you doing back? Did you leave something in here, earlier?"

"Hi Maude. No, I'm expecting a friend to join me, shortly."

"Can I get you a cup of coffee while you wait?"

She shook her head. "It's too hot for coffee. What about a glass of sweet tea? Do you have ice?"

"Sure do. The ice truck drove around to the back not more'n thirty minutes ago." On her way to the kitchen, she whirled around and looked at Gazelle. "Sugar, I reckon I got so busy trying to tend to your business I clean forgot to take your order. What can I bring you, hon?"

"I'll take a glass of sassafras tea if it's not a bother."

"Why, ain't you sweet! Ain't no bother a'tall. Coming right up."

The two strangers sitting near the window plunked money on the table and walked out the door.

Gazelle slowly sipped on her sassafras tea and cut her eyes over at the woman. Embarrassed when the woman caught her staring, she bit her lip. "Uh, I was just admiring your lovely dress. Red is my favorite color."

The woman's eyes lit up. "Thank you. I hope the one I'm wearing it for likes it." She pulled at a tiny watch chain clipped to her dress, then blew out a wisp of air. "Goodness me, I'm as nervous as a cat. Can you tell?"

Gazelle giggled. "Me, too." The woman spoke to her as if she were an adult and not a twelve-year-old kid. She hoped Miss Lady-in-Waiting would be as easy to talk to. A sudden thought caused her mouth to gape open. *What if? No, it couldn't be. Why not?* She tried to find a way to word the question, though there didn't appear to be any other way than to blurt it out. "I don't mean to be nosy but you wouldn't happen to be waiting for someone who wrote you a letter, requesting a ten o'clock meeting would you?" She caught her lip between her teeth. "Because, if you are, I may be the one you're waiting for."

The beautiful lady smiled graciously and took a sip of tea. "No, dear, but I hope your guest shows up soon. Waiting can be torturous, can it not? Actually, I'm waiting on a man, and I'm sure he has a valid reason for being late. He has several children and I understand it's not easy for him to stay on schedule."

Gazelle's pulse raced. "Would he happen to have five children?"

"You're a very good guesser. Yes, he does. Can you imagine the chaos in that household? But if things go the way I hope, I'll have a solution that will make things much easier for him."

Gazelle picked up her glass, walked over, pulled out a chair and sat down. Ignoring the woman's shocked expression, she reached across the table. "Miss Lady-In-Waiting, I'm Gazelle Marlowe. There's no need for either of us to wait any longer since we're here for the same reason."

"You? But where's—"

"My father? He's on the circuit." She threw up her hand. "Excuse me, I suppose I should explain. My father is the Reverend Castle Marlowe, the circuit rider preacher."

Elsie couldn't decide whether to laugh or cry. The bones in the corset felt like railroad spikes poking her in the ribs. *All this torture for Cass, and he sends a child?*

"I'm sure you've heard of him."

"Yes, I know your father. I was expecting him to come." Seeing the confusion on the child's face, she concluded Cass had not told her they were once very much in love. She quickly added, "What I meant to say, was I thought the writer of the correspondence would be here."

Gazelle giggled. "I wrote the letter."

Elsie sank in her chair. "You? Then . . . he doesn't know of the letters . . . or of this meeting?"

"Oh, of course, he knows. He's the one who placed the ad in the paper, but he's leaving it up to me to approve."

Now, it was beginning to make sense. "Your father is very thoughtful to trust you with such a big decision."

"Yes, he is. This is my very first time to interview someone and I suppose there are a few things I should ask you. You mentioned in your letter that you own a store?"

"Yes, it's right down the street."

"Well, if you marry my father, naturally, you would need to stay home with the children. Of course, my brother Goat and I are capable of taking care of ourselves, but the younger ones need a woman around."

Elsie's heart hammered. "Yes, I could do that, if needful since I have a very capable young lady who could run the store for me. I'll advertise for a seamstress to help her, but it will be no problem at all to work out the details. Assuming you find me satisfactory."

"I do indeed." Gazelle felt right proud of herself for sounding so mature. "Well, I suppose that's all I really need to know. You're hired." Gazelle covered her mouth and giggled. "That was much easier than I expected. I've never had to hire a wife before, but I'm sure Father will be very pleased. He really needs you. We all need you."

"Did he say that—that he needs me?"

"More than once. Would he have placed the ad if he hadn't needed you?"

"You're right. I can't tell you how excited I was when I read it. So, when will your father be back from his trip?"

"I'm expecting him mid to late afternoon."

"Today?"

"Yes ma'am. Would it be possible for you to drop by our house after you close tonight? It's the Amelia House on Route #2. Perhaps you're familiar with it?"

"Quite familiar. Everyone in town knows the house. But if it's alright with you, I'd like to drop by around three o'clock. If he isn't there by then, I'll wait for him."

"That's a grand idea. You'll want to meet all the children, and by coming early, you'll catch them before bedtime." Gazelle stood and reached out her hand. "Thank you, Miss—" She giggled. "I'm sorry, I didn't get your name."

"Elsie Drummond."

"Well, it's a pleasure, Miss Elsie. I think my father will be very pleased when he sees you. I'll be expecting you, then, at three."

Elsie left and Maude wrapped one of her pound cakes in cheese cloth and handed to Gazelle. "Be careful, hon and keep it shoved over in the far corner of the wagon, to keep the dust from flying around it."

"How much do I owe you for it?"

"Aww, pshaw, keep your money, sugar. I'll put it on your papa's tab. He'll likely be in here one day next week."

"Thanks, Miss Maude."

When she drove the wagon through the arch at Amelia House, she giggled, seeing all four of her siblings running out to meet her. Goat was holding Gopher and the twins ran along side of the wagon until she came to a stop.

Gander yelled, "Where's the cake?"

Feigning surprise, she said, "Cake? What cake?"

Goat's lip curled. "You'd better be fooling. I haven't been able to put the little monster down for a single minute since you've been gone."

"I was joking. I didn't forget. Y'all get in the house and wash up, and we'll cut it after lunch."

Gazelle sliced a loaf of bread into ten pieces, spread each piece with fresh butter, then layered five slices with thinly sliced ham before topping with the remaining bread.

Each child took their place at the table. Goat said, "How did it go? If she was ugly, I'm sure you hired her."

"You might be interested to know that she's very attractive and you'll have an opportunity to see for yourself in a few hours."

"She starts today? Don't you think Father should have a say-so in this decision?"

"Have you forgotten? He's coming back today."

"Oh, yeah. Well, that's good." Goat took a swig of milk, then wiped his mouth with the back of his hand. "Did you know her? I hope it wasn't ol' lady Lowder. I don't think I could eat her rice pudding every day and I'm not sure she knows how to cook anything else."

Gander piped up. "I agree."

Gazelle laughed. "You'd agree with Goat if he said men lived on the moon."

Goat winked at his little brother. "They do. Don't they Gander?"

Gander nodded. "Yep. And women live there too. Right, Goat?"

Gazelle said, "To answer your question, it wasn't Miss Lowder, nor the widow Matthews. I'd never seen her before. Her name is Miss Elsie Drummond and she owns a dress shop only a few doors down from Maude's. I've seen the sign lots of times but have never been inside. I seem to remember Mother saying she bought a hat . . . or maybe it was a pair of shoes she saw in the window at a dress shop in Vinegar Bend, but since she ordered most of her clothes from Paris, I doubt they were acquainted. I'm sure Miss Elsie would've said so if she had known Mother."

"Did she know Father?"

"Of course. Everyone knows of Father. As soon as you all finish your cake, I'd like for you to wash up and put on fresh clothes. We want to make a good impression. Goat, I ironed your white shirt last night. You can keep on the same trousers but use a dab of Father's hair tonic and slick your hair back. Goose and Gander, run on upstairs and I'll be up to help you after I put everything away."

Gander's lip poked out. "I want to go back outside and play."

Goose chimed in. "Yeah, we were looking for doodle bugs."

"Yes, I can tell. Now do as I say and scoot upstairs."

CHAPTER 15

At precisely three o'clock, Gazelle pulled the curtains back and peeked out the window to see a motor vehicle pulling into the yard. Goat came running down the stairs. "Jumping jellyfish, wouldja look outside. Hot diggedy dog."

Gazelle turned sharply with her finger pressed over her mouth. "Shh! Do you want her to think we're a bunch of hooligans?"

"Sorry," he whispered. "But she has an automobile. You did good, sis. I wonder if she'll let me drive it?"

Gazelle put on her brightest smile before opening the door. "Welcome to Amelia House, Miss Elsie."

"Thank you, Gazelle. And this handsome young man must be Goat?"

"Correct, m'lady." He reached for her hand and kissed it. "It's a pleasure to meet you, ma'am."

Gazelle rolled her eyes. Was this really her brother? Hiding behind her skirt were the twins. She stepped back. "And this is Gander and Goose. Say hello to Miss Elsie, children."

They mumbled shyly, then shot back into the house.

Elsie smiled. "I don't suppose your Father is home?"

"No ma'am, but it shouldn't be much longer. I'm sure you'd like to see little Gopher, but he takes a nap after lunch." She laughed. "I should say he naps if I'm lucky, and today was my lucky day. But he never sleeps long at the time, so I'm sure he'll be up, soon."

"Yes, I'd love to see him. What did you call him?"

"Gopher. That's not his Christian name, of course, but Father gave us each a nickname from the day we were born. My real name is Esther—you know, like the queen in the Bible."

"Esther is a lovely name. Would you like for me to call you Esther?"

"No thank you. I'm accustomed to answering to Gazelle."

"Oh. Then Gazelle you shall be."

Goat yelled, "There he comes."

The twins heard Goat, rushed out the door and ran toward the dust flying on the dirt road. "Father, father," they shouted.

Gazelle popped her palm to her forehead. "Miss Elsie, please forgive my manners. Won't you come inside? We can wait in the Parlor and give Father time to put up the buggy and greet the children."

"Thank you, Gazelle." She reached up and gently touched her hair. "Do I look presentable?"

"You look very nice, but Father said he doesn't care what you look like. It's what's inside that appeals to him."

Elsie bit her lip. "He said that?"

"Yes ma'am. Said it right after he told me he wanted me to go meet you."

"I have an idea, Gazelle. I'm sure your father has missed you, so why not go out and greet him, then let him know I'm waiting for him in the Parlor. To be honest, I'm a little nervous, so if you could allow us a few minutes alone time . . . you know . . . to speak as one adult to another about things he might find embarrassing to discuss in front of his children. I hope you understand."

"Of course, I understand. I'll let him know you're here." She met her father as he was walking up the steps.

"There's my girl." He embraced her in a hug. "Have you missed me?"

"I always miss you. Father, there is someone—"

"I saw the car when I first rode up, and the kids seem quite excited. Where is she?"

"Waiting in the Parlor. I'll keep the children out while you get acquainted. She's very nice. I think you'll like her."

"First, I want to know how you like her."

"I think she's perfect for you."

"It's not me I'm concerned about. I want her perfect for you kids."

"Goat likes her. Or at least, he likes her automobile. And the twins will like anyone who will fix their meals and kiss skinned knees."

He smiled. "I suppose you're right. Please let her know I'll be in there shortly. I'd like to splash a little water on my face and change shirts. With this drought going on, I've been eating a lot of dust."

Gazelle walked down the hall and opened the parlor door. Elsie was posed in front of the fireplace with one hand on the mantle, and the other on her tiny waist.

She quickly lowered her arms. "Where's your father?"

"He asked me to let you know he'll be in shortly. He's cleaning up." She stepped out and closed the door behind her.

Cass swiped his sweaty palms across his pants leg. Funny, he didn't remember being nervous when he told Nellie he'd marry her niece. And even after he met Rebekah, the differences in their ages wasn't a real concern. He was more concerned about how she might feel. So why was he shaking like a leaf, now? Was it because he hadn't expected to fall in love with Rebekah? But he did fall in love. How could he marry another woman with this ache inside him so raw?

He walked into the hall and turned to see Gazelle standing on the stairs. Goat and the twins were looking down from the top baluster. Gazelle motioned him toward the Parlor with her hand and whispered, "Go on in, Father. She's waiting."

Cass opened the door and blinked twice, seeing Elsie Drummond poised with one hand on the mantle and the other planted on her waist. "Elsie? What are you doing here?" He scratched his head and gasped. "You? You're the one who—?"

She rushed over and pushed the door closed, then wrapped her arms around his neck. "Yes, darling. I am the one. I've always been the one. I can't tell you how I've longed for this day. Your ad in the paper was so clever. I knew it was meant for me."

He reached up and pried her arms from around his neck. He turned and walked over to the window, with his back toward her. "Elsie, I am so sorry, but I'm afraid there's been a terrible mistake."

Her eyes welled with tears. "Castle Marlowe, you broke my heart once. I won't allow you to do it again."

"Elsie, I apologize if you came here under the impression that I had anything to do with this, because I promise you, I didn't."

"Are you saying you didn't put the advertisement for a wife in the paper?"

He rubbed his hand across his brow. "Yeah, I did, but—"

"You read the letter I wrote in response, did you not?"

"Gazelle read the letters to me on the phone, but I didn't pay close attention."

She burst into sobs. "Cass, you knew it was me. You had to know."

He'd been in such a hurry the night Gazelle read the letters, he didn't really pay attention to the contents. He only listened for the names, in case there was someone he knew. "How could I have known it was you? If I remember correctly, the only anonymous letter was signed with something like Maid of Honor."

"Lady-in-Waiting," she corrected. "But all the markers were there. I know you recognized it as coming from me."

He walked over to the brass hat rack, picked up her hat and handed to her. "I'm sorry you're offended. I wish it hadn't happened, but there's no way this arrangement would ever work."

"Why not, Cass?" She dabbed her wet face with a lace handkerchief. "No woman will ever love you the way I love you. The way I've always loved you."

"No, Elsie. I'm sorry, but I think you should go."

With clenched teeth, she wailed, "You preach forgiveness. Where's your forgiveness, Reverend? You're still holding a grudge because fourteen years ago when we were engaged, I told you I didn't want children. Well, I couldn't help how I felt. Wasn't it better to tell the truth than to lie to you? But, don't you see? That isn't a problem now since you have all the children you could ever want. and I have the business I always wanted."

"I'll walk you to your car."

"Please, Cass. Please don't do this. I'll do anything for you. I'll be good to the children. They already like me. I know they do."

"What about your shop?"

"That will be no problem. I'll hire a competent nanny to stay with the children while I'm at work. I'll be home every night. It can be the life we both wanted from the beginning."

He opened the door and heard the children scrambling to their rooms. "There's no need in dragging this out longer. It's time to leave, Elsie."

She grabbed her long skirt and pulling it up, ran down the hall and slammed the front door.

After the car drove away, the children came trudging down the stairs.

Goat was the first to speak. "You sent her away, didn't you? Why? She had a nice automobile."

Cass grunted. "And in your eyes, that alone was reason enough to make her a part of this family, I suppose."

"Well, it sure wouldn't hurt. Besides it wasn't just her car. She was nice." He ran his fingers through his hair, then wiped his greasy hands on his pants leg. "Don't wait supper on me. As soon as I change into my overalls, I'm going fishing."

Cass glanced over at Gazelle, who appeared to be pouting. "Sweetheart, I'm sorry. There are things you don't understand."

"I understand that Miss Elsie was perfect for us. You said you were leaving the decision up to me and everyone liked her but you." She turned and ran back upstairs.

Gander said, "Can me and Goose go back under the house and look for doodle bugs?"

Cass raised a brow. "Goose and I . . . and not with your good clothes on." He looked down into pleading brown eyes, then said, "Never mind. Go play."

He ambled up to his room, took his Bible from his satchel and headed for the stump.

CHAPTER 16

Elsie went home, took off the corset and put on a dull gray dress that allowed her to breathe. Did it matter what she wore? He hardly laid eyes on her. Well, he'd be sorry. She'd see to it.

When she walked into the shop, Rebekah said, "You're back early . . . and you've changed clothes."

Elsie ignored the comment. She trudged over to the table where Rebekah was working, picked up a hat and scowled, "What's this?"

"You like it? I tried the plume on the back, but it seemed to work better on the side. I thought I might put it on the mannequin in the window. What do you think?"

"I'll tell you what I think. I think it's the gawdiest creation I've ever laid eyes on. What were you thinking? The hat is much too small for such a large ornament."

Rebekah's voice quivered. "I'm sorry. I'll remove the plume."

"I insist upon it. Make sure you don't crush the feathers where

138

it's sewn to the hat. These plumes aren't cheap."

"Yes ma'am."

Belle and Nora, two regular customers walked through the door. Elsie pasted a smile on her face and chirped, "Welcome, ladies. I'm so glad you stopped by. I just received a new shipment of beautiful material in fall prints, yesterday. Nora, with your red hair, the amber print would look lovely on you." She turned and said, "Rebekah, show them the new pattern book from Vogue."

Nora said, "Thanks, Elsie, but I'm not looking to buy a dress. Belle and I came by earlier today and I haven't stopped thinking about the hat Rebekah was working on. A lovely pillbox with a large plume on the side. Has she finished it?"

Elsie felt a hot flush rise to her cheeks. "I do believe she's almost finished. Am I right, dear?"

Rebekah picked up the hat. "I was removing the plume, but it will only take a few stitches to put it back as it was."

Elsie said, "Rebekah takes such pains with each creation. It's a lovely hat. I can certainly understand why you couldn't resist coming back."

Rebekah fought back the tears as her fingers pushed and pulled the needle and thread. What had she done to cause Elsie to react to her with such animosity? What if she fired her? Where would she go? She finished the hat and took it up front.

Nora sat at the vanity in front of the mirror. Elsie positioned it at an angle on her head. Staring at her image in the mirror, Nora's eyes lit up. She said, "What do you think, Belle?"

Belle smiled. "I think it was made for you. It's beautiful."

Elsie gushed. "I agree. It looks very becoming on you."

After the ladies left, Elsie walked to the back where Rebekah was working on another creation. "I suppose you feel I owe you an apology?"

Rebekah shook her head. "No apology necessary."

"I know it isn't necessary, but I suppose you feel you're due one. However, I was right about the hat. The plume was much too large, but fortunately, Nora Glasscoe has never had a sense for fashion. She still insists on wearing a bustle."

Rebekah couldn't help wondering what happened between early morning and late afternoon to cause Elsie's demeanor to change so drastically. Never had she seen her employer in such a foul mood. Whatever it was, must've been devastating.

Just before closing, she found the courage to ask. "Elsie, I don't mean to pry, but I'm concerned about you. You were so happy this morning, but when you came back this afternoon, it was plain to see something had happened to cause you pain. If you'd like to talk about it, I want you to know, I'm here for you."

"Thank you, Rebekah. I'm sorry for being ill with you, earlier. And you are right. Something did happen to cause me to become upset, but I'd rather not discuss it."

"I understand. I just wanted to offer a listening ear, if you should need one."

****

Cass poured his heart out to the Lord, "God, I feel like I've failed everyone. I wasn't the husband Amelia needed, Goat is angry with me and Gazelle is deeply hurt. But how can I explain to them why Elsie was not right for us? I've made so many mistakes, but the biggest one was when I let Rebekah walk out of our lives. I think I knew from the moment I saw her there was something very special about her. Her sweet, gentle spirit, and the kindness she showed to Gazelle, even when Gazelle seemed intent on making her life miserable. I could've easily fallen in love with her, had it not been for my foolish pride. The only right thing I've done lately is to send Elsie away, yet I regret having to hurt her. Lord, I need to hear your voice and I can't seem to hear."

Then, hearing a voice in the distance, he stopped.

"Are you out there?"

He opened his eyes and chuckled, "I don't think that's your voice, Lord." He stood, walked toward the house and yelled, "I'm coming, Gazelle."

"It's dark, and I was beginning to worry."

"Sorry, time got away from me."

She handed Gopher to her father. "I made ham pie for supper. It's not as good as Aunt Jewel's, but I can't make dumplings the way she did."

"I'm sure it's delicious." With one arm holding the baby and the other wrapped around Gazelle, he walked her home.

"Father, I'm sorry I lost my temper, but I thought when you

met Elsie, you'd be so proud of me. I still don't understand why you sent her away, but I'm sure you had your reasons. I just wish she could've been the one."

"Thank you, sweetheart. The truth is, I didn't meet Elsie today. We went to school together."

"Really? She didn't mention it. I wonder why she didn't say anything. I had no idea you two knew one another."

"I know you didn't. And I *am* proud of you. I'm sure Elsie would make some man a fine wife."

"Just not you? Is that what you're saying?"

"Right. Just not me."

"But why, Father? What's wrong with her?"

"Gazelle, there's nothing wrong with her. Please let it suffice when I tell you she's not the one for us. Now, let's go inside and have a big bowl of your ham pie. I'm sure it's delicious."

Cass put the baby in his highchair in the dining room. Walking back to the kitchen, he washed his hands, then called the children to supper.

Gazelle had already set the table and taken the hot pie from the oven.

Her father sat down at his usual place at the head of the table and sniffed. "Hmm, it certainly smells delicious. And I Suwannee, if those biscuits don't look just like Aunt Jewel's. You're gonna make some man a great wife, in a few years, although I don't like to think about you growing up so fast."

The twins walked in and sat down. Cass said, "Where's

Goat?"

Gander grumbled, "Gone fishing. I wanted to go too, but he wouldn't take me."

"I promise, buddy, you and I will go fishing real soon. I've just been so busy lately, I haven't had time. But your brother is gonna be in big trouble when he gets here. He knows better than to stay out this long."

With heads bowed, Cass was in the middle of blessing the food when the front door slammed and the sound of footsteps were heard running down the hall.

"Amen!" Cass lifted his head and glared at Goat, who had attempted to sneak in. He'd taken his place at the table and with his hands folded, echoed a loud "Amen."

Cass picked up the ham pie and passed it down. "Son, the smell of earth worms at the supper table is not very appealing. Please excuse yourself and go upstairs. After you've bathed and changed clothes, you may come back down."

He stood and looked at his hands. "Yessir."

After he went upstairs, Gander said, "Is Goat in trouble?"

Cass took a biscuit from the platter and passed them to Goose. "Yes, Gander, your brother is in big trouble, but I'll deal with him after supper, "

Gazelle said, "You're always saying it isn't right to discipline at the table, because it causes one to lose their appetite."

"That's right. Pass the butter, please."

She picked up the butter dish and handed it to her father. "But that doesn't make sense to me. The dread of knowing what's coming afterward does more to take my appetite away. I spend the whole time dreading the discipline that awaits. I'd rather go ahead and get it over with and be able to eat in peace."

After supper, Cass helped Gazelle clean the kitchen. He said, "I'll dry if you'll wash. It'll give me a chance to express to you how proud I am of the way you've taken charge of the household, lately. It seems as if you've grown up overnight. Frankly, I didn't know what I was going to do when Aunt Jewel died. You've been a tremendous help, sweetheart, but I hate putting so much responsibility on your young shoulders."

She reached in a drawer and handed him a dish cloth. "Thank you, Father. That brings me to something I've been wanting to say to you."

"This sounds serious."

"It is. When school starts back for the fall session, I insist on dropping out."

His eyes darkened. "Insist, do you? Absolutely not. I won't hear of it."

"But it's the only thing that makes sense. Gopher needs me."

"Sweetheart, you worry too much. I take full responsibility for Gopher becoming such a problem. I'm afraid I've let him get by with his little temper-tantrums far too long. Naturally, I felt sorry for the little fellow. A baby needs a mother. If your mother had not—" A cup slipped from his hand and crashed to the floor.

Gazelle immediately bent down. "I'll clean it up."

"No, hon. I'll get it." She handed him a broom and dustpan.

"What were you about to say, before you dropped the cup. Something about if Mother hadn't died."

"Is that what I said?" He shrugged. "I think I was going to mention Doc saying Gopher's tummy problems was because he can't digest cow's milk. He says it's not unusual when a mother's milk dries up, or—"

"Or she dies?" She dried her hands and placed an arm around his waist. "Father, I know it hurts. It hurts me, too. It took me a long time, but I've come to terms with Mother's death. Have you?"

"I don't know what you mean."

"I'm not sure you have totally accepted her death. I've noticed twice in a matter of minutes you've hesitated, not wanting to admit she's gone. I've begun to wonder if that's not why you sent Miss Elsie away."

"No, no, honey. You're wrong."

"Am I? I think you're afraid of falling in love, thinking it would be admitting that Mother is never coming back."

"Gazelle, please let me put your mind at ease. I am well aware your mother will never be back, but I thought we were discussing Gopher's stomach problems."

Her chin quivered. "Yessir. I'm sorry if I offended you."

"Sugar, I didn't mean to sound so sharp. It came out wrong. The only thing you've said that offended me was when you mentioned dropping out of school. I appreciate your willingness to do so, but it's not necessary. God's got a plan." He smiled and winked. "I'll admit, though, I'll be glad when he reveals it."

"Pardon me, but maybe he has, and you weren't listening. Just as you aren't really listening to me."

His jaw dropped. "Is that what you think?"

"It's crossed my mind."

"Why don't we have a seat at the table, and you pour your heart out. Hold nothing back and I promise I'll listen."

He pulled out her chair and walked around to the opposite side of the kitchen table. "Now, what is it you want me to know?"

She wrung her hands. "Father, I think it's time we admit there's more to Gopher's problems besides being unable to digest milk. We both know it's the truth."

"No, no, Gazelle. He's fine. I'll admit he's an ornery little cuss, but honey, the way he spits up his milk, it makes sense that his little tummy would ache."

"I don't deny he has stomach pains. I can feel it tightening when I'm holding him, and I know he's hurting the way he rears back and screams. I understand that can make him ornery. I'm ornery when I have a stomachache. But there's something else going on. I've held enough babies at church to know he doesn't react like a typical baby his age. I don't know if it's mental or physical, but our little Gopher is not right."

"Not *right*?"

"You know what I mean. I know you do."

It wasn't that the thought hadn't crossed his mind, but he

hadn't wanted to believe it. For months he'd pushed the frightening thought out of his head. He refused to let it take root. "Honey, I know you believe what you're saying, but you're wrong. Don't you see? Gopher is a smart little booger and he's learned the best way to get what he wants is to throw a tantrum. And when he does, what do we do? We give in to him and he's won again. I realize it's my fault, but when he gets a little older and a little stronger, we'll make some changes."

Tears streamed down her face. "You aren't hearing me, but then I didn't expect you to."

With his elbows planted on the table, Cass rested his chin on his clasped hands. "Hon, I can see you're worried and I know this feels very real to you. Frankly, I think if there was anything to be concerned about, Doc would've found it."

Her brow shot up. "Really? And when did he see him last?"

"I'll agree Gopher hasn't been to the doctor in quite a spell, but we were told early on that his intolerance for milk was not uncommon. If I did agree to take him for an appointment, Doc would question why I brought him. What would I say? That he screams when he doesn't get his way? I'll tell you what he'd say. He'd tell me Gopher's not the one with the problem, but I am for not administering proper discipline. How do you think that would make me feel? I know it's my fault, but I'll deal with it in my own way."

Gazelle jerked her napkin from her lap and slapped it on the table. She shoved her chair back and in between sobs said, "May I please be excused?"

Cass reached out for her arm. "I can see this has you very upset. I'll tell you what I'll do. I'll take him first thing in the morning and let Doc Brunson give him a thorough check up, so you can feel comfortable that our little Gopher is just pulling our strings."

She bent over and threw her arms around his neck. "Thank you, Father. This is one time I'd rather be wrong than right."

CHAPTER 17

Gopher's little face nuzzled under his father's chin, as Cass hummed a lullaby and rocked him to sleep. He tried to dismiss Gazelle's concerns, but he made her a promise and he had to follow through.

What if she was right? It wasn't as if he hadn't had the same thought. He'd take him to Doc Brunson, as he promised, but after tomorrow if there was indeed something wrong with his baby boy, there'd be no more living in denial. His eyes moistened. How much more could he take?

After walking the floor most of the night with Gopher, Cass was up and waiting in front of Dr. Brunson's office at seven o'clock.

Doc drove up thirty minutes later, walked over to the buggy and woke both Cass and the baby. "Good morning! I gather you two have your nights and days mixed up."

"This is the most sleep Gopher's had in twenty-four hours. Doc, you know I'm not an alarmist and though I've tried to dismiss the concerns, I'm beginning to believe there may be something going on with Gopher, causing him to cry constantly."

"Bring him on in, Cass, and let me take a look."

After listening to his heart, running his hand down his spine, taking his temperature, checking his ears, nose and throat, the doctor handed the screaming baby back to Cass.

Gopher nuzzled under Cass's chin. "Doc, I know what you think."

"You do?"

"Yes, you're gonna tell me he's spoiled. That's what I've thought, too, but—"

Dr. Brunson held up his palm. "This baby is in severe pain. How long has this been going on?"

Cass couldn't decide if it was good news or bad. A part of him was glad that Doc agreed there was a problem, so he could come up with a solution. His knees felt like jelly. But what if there was no solution?

"Cass? How long?"

He ran his fingers through his hair. "Seems like since the day he was born, but I can't say. For sure, since his mother left . . . uh . . . drowned. He hasn't been able to keep milk down since. We've been giving him the Carnation milk formula, but it comes back up almost as soon as it goes down."

"I wish you'd brought him in, sooner. I haven't seen him in

months. Didn't it concern you that he's not gaining weight?"

The doctors sharp reprimand caused the hairs on the back of Cass's neck to bristle. "Of course, it concerned me, but the last time I brought him here, I told you he couldn't tolerate milk. I was doing everything you told me to do, so how could I expect him to gain when he wasn't keeping anything down?"

"I'm sorry, if it sounded as if that was a rebuke. It wasn't meant to be. I'm more upset with myself, than with you. I should've checked on you and the kids. But the important thing is that together, we're gonna find out what's wrong with our little man. Besides not getting nutrition, what other problems have you noticed?"

"You mean besides the constant crying?"

"There are several things that together can cause him to cry. He's hungry, he's apparently in pain, and he wants to feel safe and the only way he knows to do that is to cry until someone cuddles him. Has he been running a fever?"

Cass hesitated. "I don't think so."

"Well, he has a slight one now, though not high enough to be too concerned."

Cass looked down on his shirt and pulled out a handkerchief.

"Is that blood on your shirt?"

"Yeah, he's been having nosebleeds lately, but that's not so unusual in kids, is it? Goat has them from time to time."

The doctor bit his lip. "What about bowel habits? Anything unusual?"

"Gazelle usually changes him, but I did this morning, and his stools looked fine . . . well, maybe a bit darkish."

"That's what I was afraid of."

"Why? What does it mean?"

"He may be passing blood."

"No. There was no blood. I would've noticed. Nose bleeds, yes, but there was no blood on his diaper."

"The blood is in the stools, giving the dark color."

"How would spitting up milk cause blood in the stool?"

"It wouldn't. The spitting up doesn't cause the blood, but it's possible that the problem causing the loss of blood is related to the inability to digest food."

Cass's pulse raced. "So, what do you think it is?"

"Can't say. But I found a small growth on his mouth palate that concerns me."

"You mean like a canker sore? You think that's why he spits up his milk? Maybe his mouth hurts. Pain can make you sick on your stomach. Right?"

"No, it's not a canker sore. Cass, there's a specialist in Mobile, a Dr. Callahan, who will be able to give you a better diagnosis."

"Better diagnosis? But you haven't given me a diagnosis at all. What's wrong with my baby?"

"That's what we want to find out, Cass, but I need to call and make Gopher an appointment right away."

"Is that really necessary? I trust your judgement over any of those city doctors."

"Then trust me when I tell you Dr. Callahan needs to see this baby. I'm not qualified to do what he does, Cass."

He took a few paces across the room, while rubbing his hand over the sleeping baby's back. "Fine. If you think it's necessary. See if you can get an appointment for the first of next week, and I'll make arrangements to take him there."

Dr. Brunson picked up the phone, and after speaking with the specialist, he hung up. "Cass, he'll see you as soon as you get there."

"When?"

"Today."

"I can't possibly go today."

"You can't afford to wait. This is serious. Go home, pack as quickly as you can and get on the road. You may have to stay at the hospital for several days, so take whatever you might need."

"Doc, you're scaring me."

"Well, I'm scared, too. Now, let's not waste any more time by gabbing. I'll see that the kids are cared for. The train to Mobile leaves at ten-thirty. Be on it."

CHAPTER 18

Rebekah awoke to the sound of a frightening racket downstairs in the dress shop. It was too early for Elsie. Her pulse raced. "Who's there?" She yelled, not knowing whether to hope for an answer or hope there'd be none. Grabbing an iron, she eased to the top step and looked down. Then, hearing footsteps, she yelled louder. "Get out" I'm warning you, I have a gun."

"Rebekah? Who are you talking to? You planning to shoot someone?"

She thrust her hand over her heart. "Elsie! You almost scared me to death. It's barely six o'clock. What are you doing here so early?"

"I'm sorry I frightened you, but I was tired of tossing and turning in bed. I decided I might as well get up and come on down to finish Jolene's dress. All I lack is sewing the hooks and eyes on the bolero."

"I'll be down in a jiff. I hope you'll join me at Maude's for breakfast?"

"Sure, kid. Sounds good."

****

Rebekah noticed Elsie hardly touched her breakfast. "Was there something wrong with your oatmeal?"

Her lip quivered. "Nothing wrong with the oatmeal, but apparently there's something wrong with me." The water, which welled in her eyes, now flowed freely. She lowered her head in an effort to hide the uncontrollable tears. "Rebekah, have you ever wanted to die? To end the misery?"

"Die? I've seen some hard times, but I don't recall ever being that low. But you aren't serious, are you? You don't literally mean you want to take your life?"

"But I do."

Rebekah glanced around at the patrons beginning to fill the café. "You go ahead to the shop and I'll take care of the bill. You and I need to have a serious talk."

"Thanks. I don't want Maude to see me crying. Everyone in the room would know, if she catches a glimpse." Elsie slid her chair back and darted out the door.

Elsie was seated in the sewing-machine room, hand stitching the brown-checked bolero when Rebekah walked in with a fake-looking smile pasted on her face.

"That's a lovely dress, El, and I know Jolene is going to be thrilled. No one in town will deny that you're the finest seamstress in all of Dixieland."

"Thank you." Her voice cracked. She knew Rebekah meant well but being known as the town's old-maid seamstress did nothing to booster her feelings. She laid the bolero on the Singer Sewing Machine. "Rebekah, did you mean it?"

"Of course, I did. There's no better seamstress, anywhere."

"I'm sorry. I was thinking about what you said when I walked in this morning and you shouted that you had a gun."

Rebekah giggled. "Oh, that."

"Do you? Have a gun, I mean?"

"Of course not, but it's good to know I fooled you, just in case we ever do have a break-in. I'll use that line again."

Elsie gave a slight nod. "Oh." She picked up the bolero. "I thought you were faking but wanted to make sure." She quickly changed the subject. "Did you see the rolls of netting we received yesterday?"

"I did and I love the vivid colors. I can hardly wait to create a new line of fall hats."

Elsie made no comment. She sat holding the bolero, while staring out the window with glistening eyes.

Rebekah trudged back to the front room and switched hats on the mannequin in the store window. Whatever was bothering her friend and mentor was personal and she had no right to press her to talk if she wished for it to remain private. Still, she couldn't help wondering. Plenty of people have used the expression, "I wanted to die," when they wished to emphasize the enormity of a hopeless-seeming situation. Surely, Elsie was simply dramatizing. Or was she? She dropped the hat she was working on and hurried into the sewing room. "Elsie, we need to talk."

"I thought that's what we've been doing."

"No. I mean really talk. Talk about what's going on with you. If I sound as if I'm butting into your business, then maybe I am, but I'm worried about you. You have so much going for you— you're highly admired by folks in town, you're talented, you've built a business that brings women from neighboring counties to buy your fare, and you're an attractive woman for your age."

Elsie turned slowly and made eye contact. "For my *age*?"

"Oh, I wasn't inferring—" She grimaced. "I just meant it seems to me that most women over thirty stop taking care of their appearance. Not sure why. Maybe it's because they marry, start a family, and other things take precedent. But you, you aren't like them. I think it's grand that you care about your looks."

"You really don't understand, do you, Rebekah? Well, let me inform you. A married woman doesn't feel the need to pretend to be something she isn't. She understands she was chosen and is loved for who she is." Her jaw jutted forward, and her voice reeked with annoyance. "Not so, for us old maids. We keep plugging away, putting on the lip rouge and torturing our bodies by shoving and pinching the unwanted fat into a horrible corset. We want desperately to believe there's still hope for us—that we haven't completely lost our youth. We old biddies think if we strive hard enough to be beautiful, a man will take note and consider us wife-worthy." She burst into uncontrollable sobs.

Rebekah rushed over and threw her arms around her. "Oh, Elsie, if I said something to make you sink to such a low ebb, I deeply apologize."

"It's nothing you said." She turned her head toward to window. "Would you mind locking up?"

"Now? But it's only nine-thirty. If there's somewhere you need to go, I can stay and keep the shop open."

"No. I'm not going anywhere, but I think you may be right. It might help if I talk about it, and there's no one I feel as close to as I do you. Please lock the door. I don't want anyone coming in until I finish."

"Sure." She hurried over to the door, turned the closed sign around and locked the door.

Rebekah pulled a chair up next to the sewing machine and took Elsie's hands. "Now, let's see if together we can find a solution to whatever it is that's troubling you."

Elsie squeezed Rebekah's hands. "Are you sure you're only sixteen?"

"Almost seventeen. I wouldn't lie to you. Not that I haven't ever lied to anyone. But not to you."

For the first time that morning, a soft smile formed on Elsie's lips. "I was joking, dear. I know you're sixteen, but I was referring to your maturity. You're very wise to be so young."

"Thank you. I had to grow up fast. Now, what is it that has propelled you into the depths of despair?"

Elsie sucked in a lungful of air and slowly expelled. "It's a long story. Are you sure you want to hear it?"

"Only tell what you're comfortable sharing, but sometimes just talking things out gives us a better perspective and makes it easier to deal with."

"Okay, I'll try not to cry."

Rebekah smiled, reached in her pocket and pulled out a dainty handkerchief. "Here, take this and cry if you feel like it."

"Thank you." She held her head back and closed her eyes. "Oh m'goodness, where do I begin?" After a moment of silence she said, "I was your exact same age when I fell head over heels in love with a handsome young man at my school. There were twenty-one students—fourteen girls and seven boys. Ten of the girls were under twelve, but there were four of us between fourteen and sixteen who were crazy about this one particular fifteen-year-old boy—I'll call him Henry."

Rebekah grinned. "I assume that wasn't his real name."

"No. I don't know why I shouldn't tell you. Everyone in town old enough to remember back then knows exactly what happened."

"It's okay. We'll call him Henry. So, he was younger than you?"

"Only by a year, but he was so handsome, smart and genuinely good." She smiled. "Even the little kids followed after him, as if he were the Pied Piper. Charlotte Marko was one of the girls vying for Henry's affection. Being the most beautiful girl in all of Alabama, I was certain he'd choose her."

Rebekah turned loose of Elsie's hands and sat back in her chair. "But I'm guessing he chose gorgeous you, over beautiful Charlotte, though I'm sure that wasn't her real name. Am I right?"

She smiled through the tears. "Yes. I'll never forget the day I was walking home from school and I heard him call my name. I turned and saw him running toward me. He said his cousin was having a peanut boiling on Saturday night and he asked if I'd like to go with him."

Elsie giggled. "I don't have to guess what your answer was."

She nodded. "We went and it was the beginning of a beautiful courtship that lasted almost two years." Her chin quivered.

Rebekah hung her head. "If this is too painful, you don't have to continue."

"No, now that I've begun, I want to finish. My parents both died of scarlet fever the summer after I graduated. So, I moved in with my grandmother, who lived in Citronelle. She was a fine seamstress and made clothes from her home for men and women throughout the County."

"And I suppose when you moved, the distance contributed to the breakup?"

"No. Henry rode his horse to see me every chance he got. We planned to marry as soon as he graduated. We were sitting on Granny's front porch, two weeks away from our wedding date, when the subject of children came up. I thought he was joking when he said he hoped to have a dozen kids. I laughed and told him he might need to find him a concubine since I didn't plan to have children. Naturally, I was kidding around. But the conversation soon turned serious, and as we talked, we discovered that although the discussion began as a joke, deep down, it reflected our true feelings. It led to a huge argument and I told him I had already ordered a book entitled, Safe Counsel, which told how to determine the days I would be most likely to get pregnant. I wanted him and him only and it hurt me to know that I wasn't enough for him. I cried and told him I had no plans to become his baby machine. I know it sounds cold and callous but I wanted him to understand." Uncontrollable sobs shook her body.

Rebekah reached up and blotted Elsie's face with the handkerchief. "I'm so sorry. After that, did you reach an agreement to have children?"

She stiffened. "Of course not. Why should I have to give in? I would be the one stuck home with the dirty diapers and runny noses, while he'd be off working. Well, that wasn't in my life's goal. I knew I was as fine a seamstress as Granny, and I had big dreams of owning my own shop."

"I'm assuming he didn't change his mind, either."

"No. He walked me to the door and his words cut through to my heart. He said, 'Elsie, we should thank God for allowing this conversation to take place. Can you understand what a travesty it would've been to have married, and then discover we weren't suited for each other?' Then he kissed the back of my hand and said, 'Goodbye and Goodnight, Elsie.' I've relived that moment thousands of times."

Rebekah sighed. "Was it really goodbye or did you get together again."

Elsie rubbed her eyes. "Not until recently."

"Seriously? You're getting back together?"

"No. I had hoped, but I quickly discovered he was just as insensitive and selfish as he was that night at Granny's when he walked me to the door. I love him so much and I believe with all my heart he still loves me, but he's too stubborn to admit it." She pulled out her watch. "Thank you for letting me pour my heart out, Rebekah. I'm so glad I have you to talk to. There's no one else I would trust. Honey, if I can give you one piece of advice, it would be to think of the consequences before making a snap decision that will alter your life. Decide if it's worth the price you'll pay."

Rebekah nodded slowly. "That sounds like very good advice."

"Well, I suppose we should unlock the door and get busy. I haven't even begun with Jolene's dress and she needs it for a wedding in three weeks."

CHAPTER 19

A nurse with an attitude rushed through the double doors at the hospital. "Dr. Marlowe, I presume?"

"Yes."

Sounding like a Prison Matron about to assign a convict to a cell block, she gruffed, "The doctor will be in shortly."

Cass had no time for questions before she whisked Gopher from his arms and quickly headed down the long hall. He jerked a handkerchief from his back pocket and ran after her. "Wait! His nose is bleeding."

Walking faster and without looking back, she said, "We'll take care of it, sir. Have a seat in the waiting room and the doctor will see you after he's made the evaluation." Screaming, the baby stretched out his arms, his eyes pleading for his father.

Cass watched in agony as the heavy doors at the other end of the hall opened, then slammed. Turning to the stern-looking lady at the desk, he pleaded to go with them. "He's just a little boy and he's hurting and scared."

Slowly lifting her head, she peered at him from above her spectacles. "Please do as you were ordered, sir, and wait for the doctor. The waiting room is across the hall. Number 214."

His jaw flexed. "Do as I was *ordered*? Is this a hospital or a hoosegow?" Not waiting for an answer, he stomped into the waiting room and paced the floor, too nervous to sit.

Mumbling, he tried to comfort himself. "All babies cry. That's what they do. Some, more than others. Gopher is a cry-baby. He'll grow out of it. Nose bleeds? All kids have them from time to time. Don't they? Of course, they do. So, he spits up his milk. He was weaned too soon . . . can't tolerate milk from cows or goats. He'll outgrow it." Cass had failed to notice the waiting room was filling up with people who looked as anxious as he felt. When a nervous father-to-be tried to engage those around him in a conversation, Cass took a seat and grabbed a magazine, pretending to read.

After what seemed an eternity, a tall man with angular build and thinning red hair stood in the doorway. "Mr. Marlow?"

Cass jumped. "Yes?"

Extending his hand, he said, "I'm Dr. Arthur Callahan. Please follow me to my office."

Cass's heart pounded. The office was small with no frills. The window faced the parking lot. Not what he expected a famous doctor's office to look like. He wrung his hands. "Is my baby gonna be okay?"

"Mr. Marlowe, we've run some tests, and I am consulting with another doctor from The University of Florida. I will tell you there are some signs I'm seeing that disturbs me. I'm afraid your baby is a very sick little boy."

Cass swallowed hard. "Wh . . . what do you mean? How sick? Sick with what?"

"We don't want to get ahead of ourselves and go down the wrong track. That's why I'm bringing another doctor in on the case to see what he thinks."

"Well, let me tell you what I think. I think you doctors are giving me the runaround. Dr. Brunson looks at Gopher and says I need to let you look at him. Now, you're telling me another doctor needs to look at my little Gopher, and in the meantime, he's suffering. I think you're all working together to pad one another's pocketbook."

"I know it must seem that way to you, but we all want the same thing. We want to diagnose the problem and come up with the best solution for a cure. How did he get the bruise on his neck?"

Cass shrugged. "Who knows? With four kids passing him back and forth, I suppose it's possible it was through being handled so much."

"I see. How long has he been this pale?"

"Doctor, my little Gopher has always looked pale, but that's just his complexion. His mother was fair-skinned. I brought him here because he can't tolerate milk. If you're done here, so am I."

"Mr. Marlowe, your baby is a very sick little boy and I want to help him. Dr. Brunson also wants to help him, and I'll be meeting with Dr. Biggs from Florida. We'll work diligently to find out the underlying problem, so we can treat this child and hopefully save his life. But your cooperation is paramount."

Cass lowered his head. "Sorry, doc. I'm just upset. I don't know what I'm saying. This is all such a shock."

"Of course, it is, and I understand. I only want to make sure you realize the seriousness of the situation."

The nurse walked in holding Gopher, who immediately lunged toward his father. Cass took him and immediately the baby nestled his head up under Cass's neck.

Cass tried hard not to let the moisture seep from his eyes. Cuddling his baby, he feigned a smile. "He's a little gopher, all right. He burrows his head and thinks no one can see him." Thrusting out his hand, he said, "So, are we ready to go?"

The doctor nodded. "I've conferred with Dr. Brunson, who will be monitoring him on a daily basis. After we get all the tests back, we'll determine the route we need to take, to get this little fellow up and running. His temperature is normal, now, but if you don't have a thermometer, you can get one downstairs in Pharmacy. You'll need to keep a check and if it spikes past 101, call Dr. Brunson and he'll tell you what to do."

Cass ran all the way to the depot in hopes of catching the last train going to Vinegar Bend. He made it in time with ten minutes to spare. He took a seat in the back, hoping Gopher's crying wouldn't disturb as many people, since most passengers migrated toward the front.

He wasn't sure what the nurse gave Gopher in the hospital, but whatever it was, if he could purchase it, he'd want to buy a truckload. He slept soundly and Cass eased him down on the seat across from him. His mind wandered as he gazed out the window of the moving train. Why did his thoughts always go back to Rebekah? Why did he continue to lie to himself? He knew the answer. He fell in love with that beautiful barefoot young woman at the depot in Vinegar Bend, the moment he laid eyes on her. He had wanted to believe she felt the same thing he was feeling. He was wrong. Or was he?

He ran his fingers through his hair and tried to remember exactly what transpired that made her leave. Was it something he said? Or was he only believing what he wanted to believe, and the feeling was not mutual? She was only sixteen, for crying out loud. *Seventeen*! He realized she'd had a birthday, since meeting at the train station. Still, he was fifteen years older. What woman would want to marry an older man with five children? *She did*! But why did she leave?

His brow furrowed as he recalled the conversation that changed everything. He remembered explaining to her that the children were rebellious, but he told her he'd help her discipline them. That's when she said the children hated her and she was afraid that wouldn't change if she was put in charge of their discipline.

Cass cringed." I should've agreed that I would be the disciplinarian, until everyone adjusted to the situation. Instead, what did I do? I jumped to conclusions and by not listening to what she was trying to tell me, I ran her off." Now, that he thought about it, he realized she said nothing of leaving until he mouthed off in anger and told her it was a job for a more mature person. "Was I crazy? She was more mature than some thirty and forty-year-old women I know."

He leaned his head back on the seat and moaned. His throat tightened as he relived the moment of desperation when he made the assumption she wanted out of the marriage—*I told her to put her bag in the guest room and I'd put her on the train the next day.* She never mentioned wanting to leave. Out of his pain, he promised to have the marriage annulled. He popped his hand over his mouth. *I forgot!* He'd intended to, but other things kept interfering.

Now what! He married Rebekah while he was still married to Amelia, although Amelia had been legally declared dead. Now, he and Amelia were divorced, but was the marriage to Rebekah null and void, even though he didn't know his wife was still alive? Or were they still married? Shouldn't he find out and let her know? Shivers ran down his spine. Would she be furious to find out she married a married man or would she be angry that he promised to have their marriage annulled and failed to do so?

What a mess he'd made. He wasn't fit to be one of God's messengers. He buried his face in his hands and cried out, "Oh,

Lord, I sketch all these scenarios on a chalkboard, and preach of the cunning works of Satan, when I'm chiefest among sinners. I am both divorced and a bigamist. How can I tell others how to live their life when I've made such a mess of my own? His chalk drawing of the Pot calling the Kettle black flashed in his mind, causing a sickening feeling of consternation.

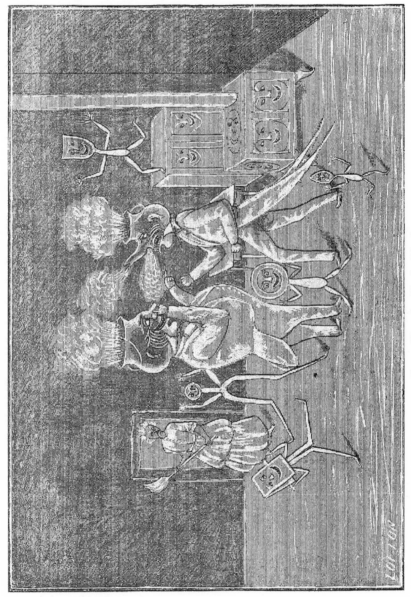

Pot calling the Kettle Black

****

Amelia Marlowe paced back and forth in the Master suite above the Goldwing Riverboat Casino in New Orleans. At three o'clock in the morning, the door eased open and Wyatt Winger crept in. She turned on a light and simultaneously threw a vase in his direction.

"You crazy woman, do you have any idea how much that vase cost me?"

"Do you think I care? You've been lying to me, Wyatt. You promised if I'd come, you'd marry me. It's been a year, and we still aren't married."

He reached out his arms, "Aww, baby, I've explained to you why we need to wait. I have a nineteen-year-old son at Harvard. He's top of his class, but he thinks his old man can do no harm."

She screamed, "So, you're saying to marry me would be harmful? Are you crazy?"

"Calm down, sweetheart. There are people downstairs. I'm saying Marcus wants to believe I'm still in love with his mother, and until he graduates, I want nothing to distract him. If he found out I married so soon after Connie's death, he'd suspect I was running around on her before she died."

"You were! It's been sixteen months since her accident—if indeed it was an accident."

"Are you accusing me of having something to do with her death?"

"I don't know, Wyatt. I don't know what to think, anymore. You helped to plan mine."

"Amelia, trust me when I tell you I love you. But I also love my son, and I won't do anything to jeopardize his future. He loves his old man, but he's never been interested in taking over the casino. He wants to be a doctor, and I'll do anything to help make his dream come true."

"What about me, Wyatt? I want to be known and accepted in this town as your wife. I want to be able to walk down the street by your side, and to attend the social events with you, instead of being stuck up here like some little—" She couldn't say it. "All you talk about is what Marcus wants. Well, what about what I want?"

His eyes grew cold. "He's my son."

"And what am I?"

"A distraction."

Her mouth gaped open. "A *distraction*?"

"That's what I said. I'm going to sleep across the hall. When I wake up, I expect you to be gone."

"No, you can't do this to me. You can't. I gave up my children for you. You promised me if I got a divorce, we'd get married."

"Yeah, I did, didn't I? I changed my mind. I didn't think you would do it. But when you did, I decided any woman who would give up her kids so freely wasn't worth having."

"Please, Wyatt. Please don't do this to me. Where would I go? I can't go back to my family after faking my death. Besides, Cass signed the divorce papers. He would never marry me again after what I did."

Wyatt threw a couple of large bills on the bed. "This should hold you until you find another sucker who will take you in. Goodbye, sweetheart!"

CHAPTER 20

Cass departed the train and walked over to the livery stable to get his horse and buggy.

Josh, the keeper of the stable, said, "Been waitin' for you to get back, Preacher. I got somebody wantin' to make a trade."

"A trade? What kind of trade?"

"Your horse and buggy for that fine automobile sittin' in front of the stable."

Cass laughed and shook his head. "That's Sam's car. I'm sure he doesn't want a horse and buggy. He worships that car."

"He did, but his ol' lady pitched a fit. She won't get in it. Says the devil's in the motor and either the car goes, or she goes." He snickered. "If it's true the devil's in it, then I 'spect he can be in two places at once, 'cause I'm pretty sure he makes his home in that woman. She's meaner than a snake. If I was Sam—though I'm glad I ain't—I know which one I'd keep."

Cass walked back out and took a look at the Model-T parked out front. He rubbed his chin. "Not that I'm interested, but what kind of deal was he asking for?"

"Your rig and two-hundred dollars. Said he paid $500."

He reached in his pocket and pulled out a bill holder. "I'll do it. I need a quicker way to travel, to get back to my children when I'm on the road."

"I don't blame you. I reckon most ever'body in town has tried to figure out why you've waited this long. If anybody in town could afford to be riding around in an automobile, it would be you."

"I had my reasons, Josh, but time changes things . . . and people. I think it's time I changed some things in my life."

Driving home, he thought about the heated conversation he had with Amelia, not long before her departure. She insisted that riding around on a horse and buggy made them appear less affluent than Sam and Lolita. It was always about appearances. He smiled, wondering what she'd think if she knew he'd bought Sam's car and Lolita would now be riding in his buggy. But he had the satisfaction of knowing he purchased it out of need, with no intent of impressing anyone.

He held Gopher in his arms, who seemed to be enjoying the outdoor air blowing in his face.

When he arrived home, the children ran to meet him, and Doc Brunson's wife waved from his front porch. After all the oohing and ahhing over the automobile, he handed out the penny candy, they were all waiting for. Gazelle reached for Gopher. "Father, we've missed you and Gopher, so much. Is he well, now?"

"I've missed you all, too, sweetie. Let me take Mrs. Brunson home and I'll tell you all about our trip when I return."

"Yessir." She giggled when Gopher burrowed his head underneath her chin. "My sweet little Gopher. You missed me, didn't you, punkin?"

Cass helped Mrs. Brunson into the car. She said, "I'll bet you haven't eaten supper, have you?"

"No ma'am, but I saw a light on at Maude's when we passed, so she's still open. I'll drop in and eat a bite."

"I fried chicken for the children and thought there'd be plenty left over for when you got home, but Goat can really put away the food."

"You can say that again. If he eats this much at eleven, I don't know if I can afford him by the time he gets to be a teenager."

The doctor was in the yard waiting, when they arrived. He said, "Welcome home to you both. I received a call from Dr. Callahan and I'm glad you agreed to take Gopher to see him. He's one of the best."

"Well, thanks to you and your wife. I couldn't have gone if it hadn't been for your generosity. I had no one in the community to call on."

"I'm glad we could help. But I'll check around and see if I can't find someone who can help you with the kids. I'm sure somewhere, there's a woman who could use the extra money."

Cass rolled his eyes. "I've found some of those. I want someone who is more concerned with the welfare of my children, than she is of money in her pocketbook."

Doc Brunson laughed. "In that case, you might want to look for a wife."

Cass stopped at Maude's. When he walked in, he looked over at the corner table and saw Rebekah sitting in the same place where he last saw her. 'Evening, Miss Rebekah.' His knees trembled. Why did he call her Miss? She was still a Mrs. How would she react when she found out the truth, and whether he wanted to admit it or not, she would eventually find out if she met a man and went to get a marriage license. The thought made him sick on his stomach. If he could do it all over again, he'd let her know exactly how he felt about her. But he couldn't do it all over again. It was already done.

She nodded politely. "Good evening, Reverend."

Maude yelled, "Preacher, I got a couple of pork chops left and the turnips are about gone, but I could get you a bowl of pot liquor and cornbread, if that'll do."

"That'll do fine, Maude. Thanks. I'd like a cup of coffee, also."

"Sorry, water will have to do. I've already washed the pot."

"Fine. I'll take water."

He walked over to Rebekah's table and fumbling with his hat in his hand, he mumbled, "Would you mind if I sat with you?"

She lifted a shoulder. "Suit yourself."

The first few moments were awkward. Then they both started to speak at the same time.

He said, "I'm sorry, Rebekah. What were you about to say?"

"It wasn't important. You go first."

"I thought you might want to know I took Gopher to the Mobile Infirmary to find out why he cries all the time."

"I thought he just didn't like me."

"No, no, no. He's a sick little boy. He cries because he's in pain."

"Oh, Cass, I'm so sorry. Who stayed with the children while you were gone?"

"Doc Brunson's wife. If my little man has to have surgery, I'll need to find someone to watch the kids. If you happen to hear of anyone, I'd appreciate if you'd send her my way."

"Yes. Yes, of course, I will. I know I wasn't around your children long, and I know you'll find it hard to believe, but I fell in love with them. They're good kids."

His lip lifted at the corner. "I'm sure you aren't including Gazelle, when you make that statement."

"Of course, I am. I never had a mother to love, but I can imagine if I'd had one, I would've resented anyone I thought might be wanting to take her place in my life."

"I think you'd be surprised at how much she's matured in these past few months. She's had a lot of responsibility placed on her lately and has had to grow up fast."

Maude said, "If you two have finished your meal, I need to

lock up."

Cass threw up his hand. "I'm leaving. Rebekah, you told me you had a job, but you didn't say where. Do you work here at the café?"

"No. I work at the dress shop."

"Not . . . not Elsie's dress shop?"

"That's the one. I owe her a lot. She hired me when I had nowhere to go and taught me to make hats."

"I see. If I'm not being too personal, where do you live?"

"I have a room over the shop. Elsie lives in the big house on the corner where she grew up, but you probably knew that already, since you grew up here, also."

He nodded. "May I walk you to the store?"

"Thank you. I'd like that."

They talked about the weather, the stars, cotton and boll weevils—everything except the one thing that occupied Rebekah's mind. Could it be he also had regrets that things hadn't worked out? Or was she only dreaming? "Cass, I'll be praying for Gopher, and for you to find someone to stay with the children. I'm sorry I wasn't what you needed."

He held his palm in the air. "It's beginning to rain. I should let you go in."

"Do you still want a cup of coffee? It would only take a few minutes to brew and I think I'd like a cup, myself."

"Are you inviting me in?"

The bottom of a cloud appeared to fall out, as rain fell in

torrents. She laughed. "Of course, I'm inviting you in. We're getting soaked, standing here."

She picked up one of her creations from a hat rack. "I'm still working on this one. What do you think?"

"I think it's lovely. And you made it?"

Rebekah beamed. "Sure did. It's fun being able to take nothing and turn it into something beautiful. Come on up, and I'll put the coffee on the hot plate."

He followed her up the stairs and took a seat on the sofa. He watched her standing at the sink, pumping water into the coffee pot. Her hair fell loosely over her shoulders. It must've grown six inches since the day I met you at the depot. Her beautiful dress outlined every curve. He'd never noticed what a tiny waist she had. But it wasn't her outward appearance that he admired most. It was the inward, wholesome beauty that intrigued him. Never had he met anyone like her.

She had been full of talk, downstairs. His knee jerked, the way it always did when he was nervous. What was he thinking, coming up here? Obviously, she and Elsie didn't confide in one another, or she would've mentioned it. Why had she suddenly clammed up. "Uh . . . Rebekah, is Elsie—" He paused and popped his knuckles. "What I mean is, do you and Elsie . . . I was wondering—" Coughing in his hand, he said, "Do you get a lot of business?"

She laughed out loud. "The way you stammered, I thought you were about to ask something personal. But in answer to your question—yes, we're doing very well. Elsie says business almost doubled after she hired me to take over the millinery."

"That's good. I suppose now that you've found something you enjoy doing, you'll probably want to have your own shop one day. I think that would be great. Rebekah's Millinery. Sounds good, doesn't it?"

She shrugged. "Not really."

"But I thought you loved what you're doing."

"I do, but it doesn't mean I want to do it the rest of my life. I hope one day to have a home and children, but until that day comes, I'm glad I have something fulfilling to do. I love Elsie, but we're different in that respect."

"How's that?"

"She's always known she wanted to have her own business, and she allowed nothing to stand in her way."

"So she told you she chose a career over home and family?"

"Yes. Maybe I'm talking out of turn, but she said she was once engaged to a wonderful man when she was much younger, but he wanted children and though they were both very much in love, the engagement was called off because she couldn't agree to be a stay-at-home wife and raise a family. I think that's a rather sad story, don't you?"

"What's sad about it? She got her wish, didn't she?"

"No, I don't think she did. I found out earlier, she's still madly in love with him. Now, do you agree that it's sad? Two loves that were meant to be together, yet neither could find it in their heart to compromise."

He took the last swallow of coffee. "Thank you for the coffee. I think I should go." He was halfway down the stairs, when he turned around and saw Rebekah standing at the top. "Do me a favor?"

"Sure. What can I do?"

"I probably shouldn't have come here tonight. I'd appreciate it if you wouldn't mention it to anyone. I'll lock the door as I leave." He quickly bounded down the stairs and hurried out the door.

Rebekah took a rag from the buffet drawer and wiped away the tears trailing down her face. For a few short moments, she actually thought he had feelings for her. It wasn't the first time she'd allowed her imagination to run wild. He not only didn't have feelings for her, he was ashamed for anyone to know that he spent time with her. Did he not understand how his words were degrading? She suddenly felt dirty and ashamed that she had allowed him upstairs. Well, he had nothing to worry about. There was no way she would ever want anyone to know.

CHAPTER 21

Cass managed to get breakfast on the table, while holding Gopher, although the biscuits were burned and the eggs were overdone. Goat held onto the egg platter, and gently moved the eggs around with his fork, eyeing each one, carefully.

"Stop playing in the eggs, son, and pass them down the table."

"I wasn't playing. I was trying to find one with a runny yellow. I don't like well-done eggs."

"Well, when you decide you'd like to start preparing breakfast, you can cook them the way you like them. But until you do, you'll eat what's put before you. Understand?"

"Sorry, Father." He slid an egg onto his plate, but his downturned lip revealed his displeasure.

A knock at the door got everyone's attention. Gazelle said, "Shall I answer it?"

Cass nodded. "Thank you."

Glaring at the elderly woman standing in the doorway and without allowing her a chance to speak, Gazelle shook her head, somberly. "I'm sorry, ma'am, even if the offer were still available, you wouldn't have met the criteria. Have a good day." The old woman smiled sweetly, and Gazelle immediately regretted speaking so callously. She leaned in and whispered, "It wouldn't have worked, anyway. You're twice his age." Instead of showing disappointment, the woman appeared amused.

Hon, would you mind if I spoke to your Father?"

"I'm sorry, he's eating breakfast, but I'll tell him you stopped by."

"But you haven't asked me who I am or why I'm here."

"Oh, I know exactly why you're here and Father relies on my judgment. I am truly sorry." She closed the door and hurried back into the dining room.

Cass said, "Who was at the door?"

"Just some old woman, answering your advertisement for a mail-order bride. I told her we didn't need anyone. That's true, isn't it?"

He cringed, hearing "mail-order bride advertisement," but that's exactly what it was, wasn't it? When a thought ran through his mind, he jumped up from the table and ran to the door. The woman was walking down the road. "Please, ma'am. Come back."

The children all shoved away from the table and ran down the hall. Gazelle pulled on her Father's shirt sleeve. "No, Father. You can't marry *her*. She's too old for you. We're doing fine."

The woman was about as round as she was tall and she waddled when she walked. Her salt-and-pepper hair was knotted in a bun on the back of her neck. She turned, and with a puzzled look, placed her hand across her large bosom. "You talking to me, sir?"

"Yes ma'am. I'm afraid there was a misunderstanding. Do you mind telling me why you came to my door?"

"Doc Brunson rode by our place last night and said I might could pick up some extra work from you from time to time. The name's Daisy Machess."

Cass heard Gazelle blow out a sigh, behind him. "Yes ma'am. I do need help. Won't you come on back and let's sit on the porch and discuss it?"

Gazelle laid Gopher on a pallet on the floor with a sock toy, and followed her siblings to the porch. The woman seemed right friendly and although the thought of her being a stepmother was terrifying, Gazelle sized her up and decided she'd make a fine housekeeper and nanny.

After introducing each one of the children, Cass said, "Kids, this is Miss Daisy Machess."

Gander said, "You're just like our horse."

She snickered. "I eat like one, that's for sure."

Cass felt a blush. "Gander, I don't think that's—"

Gander interrupted. "Our horse's name is Patches, just like yours."

Cass's mind was eased when the woman laughed so heartily, her round stomach jiggled. The jolly laugh was enough to let him know she was exactly what he was looking for. "You misunderstood, son. Miss Daisy's last name is Machess with an 'M,' not Patches with a 'P'."

Daisy patted Gander on the head. "Well, Patches with a 'P' is a fine name for a horse. I think I like it even better than Machess with an 'M.'"

Cass said, "Miss Daisy, I'm looking for someone to come in about sun-up every morning to cook breakfast and do a woman's chores. If you can have supper fixed by four o'clock in the afternoons, you can be on your way home. Gazelle can heat it up and get it on the table when it's time to eat."

"That sounds fine, Preacher Marlowe. I'll be happy to take the job."

"Wait, there's more. As you probably know, I'm a roving preacher."

"Yessir. I know who you are. You're the Chalkboard Preacher ever'body talks about. I ain't never seen you sketch one of your Bible stories, but I hear tell, it's sump'n to behold. I'd sure like to see it one day. I hear tell some of them sketches will scare a soul out of any thoughts of going to hell."

"Thank you, I think?" As I was saying, I ride the circuit and am gone over night from one to three nights a week."

Her mouth turned down. "Oh, Preacher, I'm so sorry. My husband is feeble and I couldn't possibly stay overnight, unless of course it was an emergency."

He rubbed his chin. "I see."

Gazelle, said, "Father, please hire her. We'll be fine at night while you're away. I promise I can get the children to bed on time every night and they'll sleep until Miss Daisy arrives."

He cocked his head slightly. "I don't know, hon."

"Please, trust me?"

When she put it like that, how could he refuse. He couldn't deny she was dependable. He slowly nodded. "Okay, we'll give it a try. Miss Daisy, when could you begin?"

She let out another one of her belly laughs. "If dinner ain't started, I could get in the kitchen now, and get sump'n stirred up. 'Don't mean to be braggin', but folks say I'm a pretty good cook."

Goose looked up with those big brown eyes and reached out her little hand and placed it in the rough, calloused hand of Miss Daisy.

"Oh my soul, if you ain't the sweetest little thing. I think we're all gonna git along jest fine. And where's the baby Doc spoke of, Preacher?"

Gazelle led the way into the house and picked up her baby brother. "This is Gopher. He cries a lot, but he can't help it. He doesn't always feel good."

The woman reached out short, pudgy arms. "Bless his little heart. Come to Miss Daisy, precious."

"He doesn't take to strangers. He'll have to get used to you." But almost before Gazelle could finish her statement, Gopher lunged toward Daisy's open arms.

The kids all giggled and looked at their father. Cass said,

"Well, that's a first. I believe he likes you."

"Folks say I have a way with young'uns. Don't know what it is, but they usually take to me."

School resumed and Miss Daisy was a God-send. Cass couldn't remember when he'd felt this confident. The house was clean, the meals were delicious, the children couldn't love the old woman more if she were the grandma they never had. And after seeing the maturity in Gazelle, he was confident she could handle anything that might arise at night during his absence. She had become a surrogate mother to Gopher and Cass hated she had to get up in the middle of the night with him, but she was happy the way things were, and never complained about loss of sleep. Having Miss Daisy there, allowed Gazelle to spend time studying in the afternoons, instead of worrying about chores. If Gopher had a particularly bad night, she could even take a short nap after school, before beginning her homework.

Things were working out much better than he could ever have anticipated. Daisy Machess was truly an angel. Gopher was no better, but he was no worse, and Cass believed that to be a good sign. The fear and anxiousness that he went through at the hospital had lessened and it felt good getting back on track with his Chalkboard Ministry.

CHAPTER 22

Cass paced the floor Monday morning, waiting for Miss Daisy, though she still hadn't shown up at a quarter past six.

Gazelle assured him he was worrying needlessly. Miss Daisy would be coming shortly, and he should be on his way. "If she's much later, I'll send the kids on to school, and I'll wait here with Gopher until she shows up. Please go, and don't worry about us. We'll be fine. She's a little late, but she's very dependable and I'm sure she'll be here soon."

He chewed the inside of his cheek, mulling over his options. To stay would be to undermine Gazelle, at a time she needed to be assured he trusted her. "I'm so proud of you, sweetheart. I'm not sure I tell you enough how proud I am of the way you've pitched in and handled things in such an adult manner."

"Thank you, Father. Now, scoot. You've wasted enough time, here." She stood on her toes and kissed him on the cheek. "I'll see that everyone is fed, and we'll make school lunches together, if Miss Daisy isn't here in time to do it for us. There's nothing to worry about."

He nodded half-heartedly. "You're right." He threw his bag on the rumble seat and rode off. If he was doing the right thing, why did it feel so wrong?

Gazelle waited all day for Miss Daisy, and as soon as the children came home from school, she told Goat to watch the little ones, while she rode Patches into town. "Miss Daisy never showed up. I'm sure there's something wrong or she would've been here."

He picked up an apple from the basket on the kitchen table. "Are you going to the Fall Picnic with Jeremiah?"

Her jaw dropped. "What makes you think I'd be going with Jere?"

He giggled. "Because you love him. I heard you telling him when you met him down at the creek."

Her brows squished together. "You were spying on me."

"No, I wasn't I was around the bend, fishing. I couldn't help what I heard."

"So, help me Goat, if you ever tell—"

"Aw, stop fretting. I don't plan to tell. Besides, I got me a girl."

"No, you don't."

"I do so. Katie Nichols slipped me a note in class and asked if I liked brownies or pecan pie best."

"That doesn't mean she's sweet on you."

"Does, so. She told me her basket would be pink with a green ribbon tied on the top, so I'd know which one to pick."

Gazelle smiled. "Well, I like Katie. But you know you'll have to dress up."

"I don't care, although I'm sure I've outgrown my coat. I haven't worn it in months."

"You're almost as tall as Father. Maybe you could wear his, but I thought you hated dressing up."

"I do, but not if it means I get to go sparking with Katie Nichols."

"You'd better not ever let Father hear you talking like that. He'll tan your hide. But I can't stand here talking all day. I need to go."

"Do you even know where Miss Daisy lives?"

"No, but Doc Brunson will. He's the one who sent her to work here."

"I hope you won't be long. The fellows are playing ball in the pasture, this afternoon."

"I promise to hurry. Keep everyone out of the parlor. Gopher's sleeping and he's been very cranky, today."

Tossing the apple core into the nearby trash bin, he said, "Don't worry. I'll keep the twins outside until you get back. I don't want the little monster to wake up on my watch. But if you're going, get gone. It gets dark earlier now, and I want to have daylight left so I can play ball."

"I can't guarantee you what time it will be, but trust me, I don't want to be out past dark any more than you want me to be. I have no idea where I'll have to go to find Miss Daisy, after I get there. In case I don't get home in time for supper, there's soup on the stove."

"Well, stop batting your gums and get going."

Gazelle went to get the horse from the barn and was saddling up when Goose ran over. "Sissy, I'm itching, and I've got little red bumps on my arm."

"I'm sorry. I'm sure it's mosquito bites. They're bad this time of year. Run play, and I'll be back as soon as I can."

Goat walked outside with two apples and tossed them to the twins. "Sissy is gone to town and Gopher is asleep and I want him to stay that way until she gets back, so I need you both to play outside. Understand?"

They both nodded. Goose said, "I don't wanna play. I don't feel very good."

"Stop whining, Goose. You're fine. I don't want you in the house until you see Gazelle riding up."

He skipped up the stairs to his room. Standing in front of the mirror, he flexed his muscles, then bent in and looked closer at his face. "I'll be John Brown, I'm growing a beard. I can see it when the light hits my face."

"You don't have a beard." He turned to see Goose standing in the doorway. "Get out of here. What did I tell you about coming in the house?"

"Can't help it. I'm itching."

"Then scratch."

"I mean all over. Look."

She held out her arms.

"That's just great. You've gotten into some poison ivy. Come on in the kitchen and I'll pour a little vinegar on a rag. Rub it everywhere you itch."

"All right." Her lip quivered. "Can I stay inside if I lay down on my bed and promise to be quiet?"

"I reckon. Just make sure you stay there."

****

Gazelle rode straight to Doc Brunson's. There was a note on the door. "Closed. I'm taking the wife to stay with our daughter in Pensacola to help with our new grandbaby. Be back in a day or so. Doc."

She hitched the horse up to a post and walked across the street to Maude's. Maude yelled from across the room, "Have a seat anywhere. I'll be with you d'rectly." Gazelle said, "I didn't come to eat, Miss Maude. I'm needing some information. A woman named Miss Daisy has been working for us, but she didn't show up today, and I'm worried about her. I don't know where she lives, so I thought maybe you might know. I plan to go check on her."

"You mean Daisy Machess. I sure do know, sugar. She's my sister-in-law, but you don't wanna go to her house. Poor Daisy has the chicken pox and it's highly contagious. I talked to my brother last night and he said he ain't never seen Daisy that sick in her life. I 'spect she never got them as a child. It's unusual for a grown-up to get infected, unless they ain't never had 'em."

Gazelle's voice quaked. "She won't die . . . will she?"

"Now, that's not for me nor you to determine. It's up to the Good Lord. But it wouldn't surprise me. Poor ol' Daisy has always been a hard worker, but it's about caught up with her. She has a rough time gettin' around, though she does her best to hide her infirmities."

"Thank you, Miss Maude. The next time you talk to your brother, please tell him to let her know we're very sorry and will remember her in our prayers."

"I'll do it, sugar. Now, you best get on home before dark sets in."

"Yes'm, I plan to do that." It wasn't until she mounted her horse that the horrifying thought came to her. *That wasn't mosquito bites—poor little Goose has the chicken pox!*

She pulled the reins and stopped the horse. "Whoa!" Bowing her head, she prayed for Goose, little Gopher, Miss Daisy, and wisdom to know what to do until her father returned. She lifted her head and saw the sign above Elsie's shop. Remembering how kind she seemed, Gazelle was sure she'd know what to do. The shop was closed, but seeing a glimmer of light upstairs, she pounded on the door.

Rebekah heard the racket and hurried downstairs, yelling, "Hold on, I'm coming."

Gazelle didn't know which one of them was the most surprised. Rebekah jerked open the door. "Gazelle! What brings you here? Is your father well?"

"Yes, but what are you doing here?"

"I work for Elsie, and she lets me live in the small apartment upstairs."

Gazelle poured out her story, telling about her father's absence, Miss Daisy's chicken pox, and her suspicion that Goose was also infected.

Rebekah's pulse raced. "When does your father get home?"

"He just left today to be gone three nights. He thought Miss Daisy was just late. We didn't know she wouldn't be coming."

"I see. Hold on, and I'll go with you."

"Thank you. Gopher is not doing well, and I don't know how to help Goose." She broke into sobs.

"Let me run upstairs and grab a few things and write Elsie a note to let her know I'll be out for a few days."

"Thank you, Rebekah, and I'm sorry I was hateful to you when you married Father. I wish you were still married to him."

"Your father's a good man. I wish it had worked out, also."

Gazelle cried. "It was all my fault."

"No, Gazelle. It was no one's fault. It wasn't meant to be." She picked up a pen and wrote a note on the back of a charge pad:

Dear Elsie, an emergency has come up and I won't be able to come in to work for a few days. Will be back as soon as possible. Rebekah.

CHAPTER 23

Goat lay across his bed with his Literature Book and tried to concentrate on the required reading assignment for homework. But all he could think about was beautiful Katie Nichols. The way she tossed her chestnut-colored hair over one shoulder with a slight jerk of her head. He smiled at the comparison to Patches, the way he swished his tail. Not that she reminded him of a horse, although that wouldn't be a bad thing. Patches was about the prettiest horse around. Fastest, too.

He thought about what Gazelle said about it being a dress-up affair. Who in tarnation came up with that idea? It was a picnic, for crying out loud—not a formal dinner. He slid off the side of the bed, went to his closet and pulled out his Sunday coat. He hadn't worn it since his mother died. He was glad his father didn't make him wear it to church. He slid his arms through the armholes, looked in the mirror and gasped. Just as he thought. The sleeves were a good three inches too short, and the shoulders were much too tight. He recalled the postman saying, "Young Goat, you're growing like a weed. I'll bet you're as tall as your father, now."

Goat figured he was being polite, since he lacked another inch or two being as tall. But since Gazelle had said practically the same thing, he went into Cass's room and searched his closet for the blue coat with the fancy stitching. Concluding his father had taken it with him, he pulled out a black one and tried it on. Almost a perfect fit. If he turned the sleeves under and stood with his chest out, it almost looked as if it did fit. He gazed in the mirror and marveled at how grown-up he looked. He stuck his hands in the pockets and struck a pose. He felt something in one of the pockets and pulled out folded stationary. His throat tightened as he read:

Dear Cass,

Well, I can only imagine your shock to learn that I am indeed alive and well. I have attempted to write you several times, but there seemed no way I could adequately explain why I had to do what I did, but I now have a compelling reason to attempt this difficult letter.

Goat stopped. It sounded like—no, that would be impossible. He continued to read.

Ashamed to admit to you that I scrupulously planned my demise, I considered insisting I was knocked out and lost my memory—or that I was kidnapped, or that—well, you get the picture. But you always knew when I was lying. The truth is, I married you because you are the best-looking man on the Planet, and I'm a very vain woman. I liked showing you off.

His hands trembled.

I've always wanted the best of everything, and I knew I had the best with you, but I learned quickly I was not cut out to be a Preacher's wife or a mother. After Gopher was born, I realized I cared more about me than I did the five children I bore you. That confession sounds cold, but you and I both know it's the truth. Cass, for years, I wanted out, but I cared for you too much to ruin your ministry by asking you for a divorce. I suppose there's a little good in the worst of us.

He screamed. "Liar, liar. You're both big fat liars!"

Goose crawled out of bed and walked across the hall. Standing in the doorway, she said, "Who were you talking to, Goat?"

"Myself. Go back to your room."

"I don't feel good."

"Stop complaining, Goose." He strode over and slammed the bedroom door. A part of him wanted to finish reading, but another part wanted to run away. Everything he had believed was a lie. Unable to stop himself, he read the next page.

Now, things have changed, Cass, and I feel it only fair to tell you what happened, though it pains me to admit—even to myself— what a bad person I am.

I planned this for months in advance and had secretly been stashing away cash, knowing I would need the money. You were always generous and never questioned the withdrawals. I ordered two straw hats from a mail-order catalog, and after you left, I told Bertha, the town gossip, that I was meeting an old friend at the train station. I told her we planned to take a boat ride down the

Escatawba and picnic on the island. I knew she'd be more than happy to spread the false story, giving credence to my death. I left Aunt Jewel with the young'uns and told her I'd be bringing a guest home for supper.

Angry tears ran like a flowing well down the sides of his face. "I loved her, and I thought she loved me." His vision blurred, and he wiped his eyes with the sleeve of his father's coat, before continuing.

I packed a bag and snuck it on the buggy, along with the two straw hats I purchased. I went down to the river and took our boat and several miles down the river, I tossed out the hats, then continued until I reached Pascagoula. At nightfall, I paddled to shore, then shoved the boat back into the water. With my bag in hand, I walked the train tracks to the nearest depot, where I bought a ticket to New Orleans. I can't explain the eerie feeling that came over me when I read about my tragic drowning a few days later in the newspaper. It was a perfect plan. I was finally free from the shackles binding me, and I'd been able to pull it off without harming your ministry.

Cass, I know you loved me and I thought it would be easier for you to think of me as dead, rather than know the truth. However, I've found someone who wants the same things from life that I want. He's not Mr. Perfect, like you, but he's a wealthy man and can support me in the fashion to which I have become accustomed. We're perfect for one another and he wants to marry me, but he refuses unless I can present a writ of divorcement.

Therefore, I'm enclosing divorce papers, and I'm sure you'll have no problem signing them. Please mail papers to the Goldwing Riverboat Casino, 2284 Waterford Walk, New Orleans, c/o Owner. No one need know I'm alive, and I say that not for my sake, but yours. It's better for your flock to continue believing your loving wife drowned than discover you're a divorced man.

Well, there's nothing more to say, dear one, except I'm truly sorry for the pain I have put you through. You didn't deserve it, but I was already drowning in boredom and had to find a way out. I'm convinced I made the right decision for both our sakes.

Sincerely,

Amelia

Goat jerked off the jacket and slung it on the floor. He's as big a liar as she is. He let us go on thinking she was dead. And he didn't just lie to us. He's pretending to be a fine, upstanding Christian widower when he's nothing but a low-down, two-faced divorced liar. I hate him."

He looked out the window and realized the sun had gone down. Stomping down the stairs, he went into the kitchen to heat up the soup. After ladling it into three bowls, he yelled for Goose and Gander to get to the table.

Goose shuffled down the stairs, whining. "I feel sick."

"For goodness sake, Goose, you act like you're dying. I know poison ivy itches, but there's no need in carrying on the way you do."

"I'm not hungry."

"Suit yourself." He went to the bottom of the stairs. "Gander, are you up there?"

There was no answer. "Goose, have you seen your brother?"

"No, I've been in bed all afternoon."

He realized he hadn't seen Gander since they first got home from school. His heart pounded. Gopher? He had never gone this long without crying. What if he was— He wouldn't let himself think such a horrible thought. Racing to the parlor, his throat tightened, seeing an empty pallet. Was it possible he could've crawled out the door? He ran outside and down the porch steps, yelling, "Gander? Gopher?"

"Why are you yelling at us Goat?"

He turned to see Gander pushing back and forth on the porch swing and Gopher stretched out beside him with his head in Gander's lap.

"You ran past us. Didn't you see me?"

"No. I couldn't find you. Why are you sitting out here with Gopher, in the dark?"

"He was crying and crying and crying and you told me to stay outside. I didn't know where you were, so, I picked him up, but I came right back outside, honest. I started swinging him and he calmed down. Where were you?"

"I was in my room with the door shut. I didn't hear him. I'm sorry I yelled at you. Come on inside and eat supper."

Goat picked up Gopher, and Gander slid out of the swing and ran to the kitchen.

Gander said, "Where's Goose?"

"Upstairs. She's not hungry." He took Gopher upstairs, changed his diaper and tried to get him to eat a little oatmeal, but gave up when the baby kept dozing off.

As he eased Gopher into his crib, he heard the sound of horse hoofs and pulled the curtains back. He leaned closer to the window and could tell there were two people on Patches.

He ran downstairs just as the front door opened. "Rebekah? You're back? Did you and Father work things out?"

Gazelle rolled her eyes. "It isn't what you think, Goat. She's here to help until Father returns. How's Goose?"

"Complaining. I think she got into some poison ivy, and you'd think she's dying."

Rebekah said, "May I see her, now?"

"Sure, but she may be asleep. I think she was too sleepy to eat supper."

Rebekah followed Gazelle up the stairs, but Rebekah stopped her from going into the room. "If she does have chicken pox, it can be very contagious if you've never had them."

"I don't know if we've had them or not."

"In that case, I should be the only one coming into her room. I had them when I was about the same age as Goose." Rebekah tiptoed in and placed her hand on Goose's forehead. Goose lay lethargic, with tiny red blisters all over her body.

Gazelle stood on the other side of the door. "Rebekah, how is she?"

"She's a very sick little girl. Could you please run cold water in the tub for me? I need to get her fever down." She quickly undressed the child. "You wouldn't happen to have any ice, would you?"

"Yes. I'll get some from the ice box. How much do you need?"

"Enough to put a chill in the water."

Goat stood beside his sister and yelled through the closed door. "I hope you don't plan to put her in a tub of freezing water. She'll catch pneumonia. I can't let you do that."

Rebekah said, "Goat, this is the only way to get her fever down. We have to cool her off. Now, please, don't argue. I know what I'm doing."

"Okay, but I don't like it, and I don't think Father would, either."

Gazelle said, "Goat, stop arguing and help me. Fill the tub and I'll go get the ice."

"Do either of you know which town your father is in? I think we should try to get a message to him. I'm sure he'd want to come home."

Goat shrugged. "He might've said, but I don't remember."

Gazelle said, "Me, either, but I'm sure he told Daisy."

Rebekah lifted Goose from the cold water and wrapped a towel around her. Gazelle stood at the foot of the stairs and yelled up. "Do you need anything, Rebekah?"

"Yes, please put dry oatmeal in a bowl and mix a little water with it."

"Sure. I'll cook some and add lots of sugar. Goose loves sugar in her oatmeal."

"I'm sorry, I don't want it cooked. Just add enough water to dry oatmeal until you have a paste. It isn't for eating, it's to keep her from itching so bad."

Goat said, "I'll do it."

"Thank you, Goat. You are both a big help. Where's Gander?"

Gazelle said, "I haven't seen him. I'll go check on him." She walked past his room and heard sniffling. "Hey, buddy, what's wrong?"

"Everybody is helping Goose but nobody's letting me help. She's my sister, too. I'm afraid she's gonna die."

"Well, we're all doing everything we can to help her, and you have the most important job."

"I don't have a job."

"Sure, you do. Your job is stay in your room and be her Prayer Soldier."

"What's a Prayer Soldier?"

"It's the one who stands guard and prays for the enemy to be defeated. Hold on, and I'll go get your armor."

Though Gazelle knew Gander had no idea what she meant, the tears dried, and he seemed pleased to have an important job to do. She ran to the kitchen and picked up a small, tin boiler and grabbed the fire poker from beside the fireplace. She went back upstairs and found him waiting eagerly at his door.

"Whatcha gonna do with those things?"

"Every soldier needs armor and weapons." She turned the boiler upside down on his head and handed him the poker. "Now, we're counting on you to pray against the chicken pox, and your sword is to remind you that a Prayer Soldier is the strongest soldier in the whole wide world. Can you handle your duty, Major Prayer Soldier?"

He grinned and saluted. "Yes ma'am." He marched around the room with his shoulders back, singing "Onward Christian Soldiers. Going out to war." He stopped and looked at himself in the armoire mirror. "I do look like a soldier, don't I?"

"Yes, you do. Now, I need to get back to my post, in case Rebekah needs to call on me."

Goat said, "Rebekah, I made the paste and I'm putting the bowl outside the door."

She sat Goose in the chair, opened the door and said, "You did a great job. It's perfect. Thank you, Goat."

"Yes ma'am. Can I do something else?"

"That will be all for now. I'll smear this on the blisters and I'm sure it will make Goose feel much better."

She picked up the sick little girl, laid her in the bed and gently rubbed her body with the oatmeal. "Please, dear God, please don't let her die. Help me to know what to do." She tiptoed to the door and peeked out. Goat and Gazelle were sitting in the hall, playing a game of cards. "Would one of you happen to know if your father keeps aspirin powders in the house?"

Goat jumped up. "There's a bottle in the window in the kitchen. I'll go get it."

"Wonderful. And please bring a teaspoon and a glass of water."

Gazelle said, "I'll get that."

Rebekah took the supplies, went back to Goose's bedside and lifted her head. "Take this, sweet girl. It'll make you feel all better." She eased the spoon into the little girl's mouth and tried to contain her tears.

CHAPTER 24

Gazelle and Goat plopped back down on the floor in the hall and picked up their cards. Goat said, "Do you ever wish Mother and Father were still married?"

"Of course."

He shuffled the deck. "Do you think they loved each other?"

Gazelle picked up her cards and arranged them, careful not to let her brother see. "That's a silly question."

"No, it's not. Just because two people marry, it's no sign they're in love. Like ol' man Deming and that hag he's married to."

She giggled. "Shame on you, Goat Marlowe. That's rude and Father would take the strap to you if he ever heard you say such a thing."

"Just because you don't say it, doesn't mean you don't think it. You think it, don't you, Sissy?" He chuckled. "I know you do. I wonder if they were in love when they married, or if they got married because they knew no one else would have them."

"You're so funny. But that certainly wouldn't have been true with Mother and Father. She was so beautiful and he's still a handsome man, even if he is past thirty."

"I still wonder if they were ever in love."

"Why are you talking like this?"

"Because I gotta know. I didn't think much about it when it happened, but I remember one time I was fishing down at the river. About five-hundred feet from the dock, there's a spot where I've been catching a lot of crappy. I hardly ever throw a hook in there that I don't pull up a fish. Nobody knows about it but me. It's an eddy with a deep hole right at the bend of the river, hidden by a clomp of reeds, so even when a boat passes, they don't see me."

"What are you getting at?"

"So, one day, I go down there, and I see Mother talking to a man wearing fancy white clothes, and he had a big, fine boat docked at our ramp."

"Why are you sounding so mysterious?"

"Just pondering."

She rolled her eyes. "Who was he, because I'm sure you asked."

"Mother said he was a stranger, asking directions. I didn't think much about it at the time, but looking back, I'm pretty sure with a boat like his, he knew exactly where he was. They were laughing and carrying on like ol' buddies, until they saw me. Gazelle, I don't think he was a stranger. And you know something else? The next day, Mother went missing. Don't you think that's odd?"

"You know what I think? I think you're missing Mother and you subconsciously want to have a reason to be angry with her for dying and leaving us. I understand. I miss her, too."

His jaw jutted forward. "No, you don't understand. You don't understand a thing I'm trying to tell you."

She plopped a card down on the floor. "Why are you acting so weird? Stop gabbing and play cards."

Goose drifted off to sleep, and Rebekah kept checking her forehead until she was satisfied that the fever was down. Slipping out of the room, she told Goat and Gazelle it was time to put up the cards and go to bed. She went into Gander's room and found him with his clothes on, asleep on his bed. *I should've seen to it that he had his pajamas on and tucked him in. Poor baby.*

She stopped by Cass's room and looked in on Gopher, who was sound asleep. She noticed a peculiar bruise on the side of his neck. What else could go wrong? Seeing Cass's jacket on the floor, she tiptoed in and hung it in his closet.

Then tapping on Gazelle's door, she said, "I'm going to try to see if anyone knows your father's whereabouts. I'm sure he'd want to be here if he knew what was going on."

"Where are you going?"

"I don't know, but I have to try to locate him."

"I don't want you to go. What if Goose gets worse and dies?"

"We'll pray that doesn't happen, Gazelle. Her fever is down, and I believe she'll sleep until I return, but I don't feel I should wait until morning. Go on to bed and get some sleep."

"Shall I get Goat to hitch up Patches for you?"

"No, I can do that. I'll be back before y'all wake up."

Rebekah rode into town and the only thing open was the saloon. Seeing a light on in Elsie's house, she hitched Patches to the nearest post, then ran and knocked on the door.

Elsie peeked out through the stained glass and quickly jerked the door open. "Rebekah, what's wrong?"

"It's a long story, I left you a note at the shop. I'm in big hurry and will explain later. Do you happen to know Mrs. Daisy Machess?"

"Yes, I don't know her well, but I have seen her around town. Why?"

"I'm sorry, I don't have time to explain, but I need to get to her house. Would you happen to know where she lives?"

"I think she lives over near the stockyards in a little log cabin."

"Thanks, Elsie. I'll explain everything when things settle down. I'll be back at work as soon as I can."

"Sure, hon. Take as long as you need."

Rebekah knew exactly where the log cabin was. She recalled admiring the well-swept yards and the neatly lined tin cans filled with healthy-looking plants on the front porch, the day Cass drove her from the depot to Amelia House.

The lights were all off, when she arrived. Beating on the door, she waited. Then seeing the flicker of a light, an elderly gentleman came to the door, holding an oil lamp.

"Are you lost, Miss?"

"I don't think so. Is this where Miss Daisy lives?"

"It is. Can I help you?"

"Is it possible for me to see her? I won't take long. I have one question and she's the only one who can help me."

"I'm sorry, miss, but my wife ain't able—"

A weak voice said, "Who is it Lum?"

Rebekah responded. "I'm needing to find Preacher Marlowe, ma'am. His little girl is very sick."

"Lum, ask the young lady if she's had chicken pox. If she has, bring her on in."

"I heard her, and yessir, I had them when I was little."

He led her into a small room.

"Miss Daisy, I hate to disturb you, but my name is Rebekah and I need to let the preacher know that Goose has a real bad case of chicken pox. I reckon you caught yours from her. But I don't know where he is." She wiped the tears streaming down her cheek. "I'm sorry. I'm not much of a crier, but I'm tired and I'm scared."

"Bless your heart, darlin', you have no need to apologize. Lum, look in my apron pocket and give her that little slip of paper. It has the number of the hotel he's staying at."

Mr. Machess walked over near the sink, where an apron hung on a nail. He reached in the pocket and holding out a small slip of paper, said, "I reckon this is what she's talking about."

She glanced at the name of the hotel and phone number. "Yessir. Thank you."

Rebekah rode back through town and planned to stop at Elsie's to use her phone, but when she saw the lights were out, she decided it best to wait until she got to Amelia House to make the call.

The trip back seemed much further than the trip to town. She put Patches in the barn and hurried into the house. Gazelle heard her and came running downstairs. "Did you find Father?"

"No, but I have his number. Why aren't you in bed?"

"I couldn't sleep."

"Did Goose wake up?"

"No, and neither did Gopher."

"That's good." She picked up the phone and put in a call to Leaksville. A man answered the phone. "Grover Jones, speaking."

"Mr. Jones, I'm trying to locate a preacher who is staying there. His name is—"

He chuckled. "I know his name, missy. He's sitting here next to me having a cup of coffee."

"Could I speak to him, please?"

Cass answered the phone. "This is Castle Marlowe."

"Cass, this is Rebekah."

"Rebekah? How did you know where to reach me?"

"It's a long story, but you need to come home. Goose has chicken pox and she's very sick."

"Okay, I'll leave immediately. Where are you?"

"I'm at your house. I'll explain everything when you get here." She hung up, turned around, and felt Gazelle's arms wrapping around her. "I'm so glad you're here, Rebekah. I don't know what I would've done if you hadn't come."

"I'm glad I'm here, too. Your father is on his way home."

"Then, I'm going to bed. I can sleep now, knowing you're here and Father will be back soon. He has an automobile. Did you know that?"

"No, I didn't. That's nice. Goodnight, Gazelle, and thank you. You were a big help to me, today."

"Really? Will you please tell Father when he gets here? I want him to know."

Rebekah followed her upstairs. She eased in Goose's room and gently placed her hand on the child's forehead. Her skin felt a little warm, but nothing compared to the way she felt earlier. It was too soon to give Goose another dose of aspirin, but she'd keep check and if the fever spiked, she'd wake her up and wash her down with cold water.

The minutes drug by as she waited for Cass. Her heart pounded when she finally heard a car pulling into the yard.

She ran out the door and he was already out of the car and running toward her. Whether he grabbed her or she grabbed him,

Rebekah couldn't remember. It was a blur. She only knew she was in his arms, squalling and he was holding her tight and telling her everything would be alright. She wanted to believe him. Oh, how she wanted to believe him.

He said, "Let's go upstairs. I want to see my little Goosey Girl."

"She's been so sick, Cass."

He walked in and sat on the side of her bed. Goose slowly opened her eyes. "Father? You're home."

"Yeah, baby girl. I'm home. How do you feel?"

"Not so good."

Rebekah said, "I gave her a dose of aspirin earlier, but she can have more now."

"Were you here before Miss Daisy left?"

"Miss Daisy also has chicken pox. It's a long story. I can hardly believe it's all happened in less than twenty-four hours."

He bent down and kissed his little girl's cheek. "Before she goes back to sleep, I'd like to take her temperature. Where's the thermometer?"

"Thermometer?"

"Yes, didn't you see it, next to the aspirin?"

"No. Goat brought the aspirin up. I didn't know you had a thermometer."

They walked downstairs together, and Rebekah waited at the kitchen table while Cass ran back upstairs.

When he returned, he pulled out a chair and sat down. "I'd say you've done a great job, Nurse Rebekah. I think my little sweetheart is gonna be fine."

"I hope the other kids don't get it."

"Gazelle and Goat had the chicken pox at the same time. Gazelle was three and Goat was two. Then Gander had a slight case when he was eighteen months old. I thought Goose would catch it from him, since they were inseparable. Now, I wish she had, and it would be over with. Gopher is the only one who hasn't had them. How is he doing?"

"It's strange, but he's slept a lot today. Hasn't cried much."

"That's a good thing. Poor little fellow has been through a lot. Maybe he's growing out of it."

Rebekah stood. "I'm glad you're home. I should go. Would you mind if I borrowed Patches?"

"Don't go. It's late and the Guest Room is empty. Please stay."

"I don't know, Cass."

"I need you, Rebekah."

That's all it took. "Then, I'll stay. It has been a very long day. I think I'll turn in."

"Since Amelia chose to sleep in there, you'll find nightclothes in one of the drawers."

"Thank you. It will feel good to get out of these clothes."

CHAPTER 25

Cass awoke to the smell of smoked ham wafting from the kitchen. He hurried down and saw Rebekah standing at the stove, wearing the robe he had given Amelia their last Christmas. Never would he have thought that one day another woman would be cooking in his kitchen, wearing that red quilted robe. Neither would he have imagined that he would be a divorced man, longing to hold the young Rebekah McAlister in his arms.

But she wasn't Rebekah McAlister, was she? He grimaced, wondering how furious she would be upon learning he had never had the marriage annulled. After this long a time, would any judge agree to an annulment or would they be forced to divorce. All the fears disintegrated the moment she turned around and their gaze met.

"Good Morning, Sunshine. You're up early." He walked over and picked up a small slice of ham.

Rebekah playfully swatted his hand. "Keep your paws away from the food, Cass Marlowe."

"It was just one little piece," he said while swiping his fingers across her apron. "I'll go check on the children. I'm hoping we may be over the hump. Both Goose and Gopher slept through the night."

She giggled. "So did their father."

"What do you mean?"

"I was up with both children."

He slapped his palm to his forehead. "I'm so sorry, Rebekah. I didn't hear either of them."

"Goose was miserable. I rubbed her down with oatmeal, but at least her fever was gone. Gopher was gnawing his fist, as if he were starving, but when I tried to give him the formula, he wouldn't take it. I fixed a bottle of sugar water and he drank the whole bottle and went to sleep in my arms."

"You carried him to the kitchen? Are you saying you came into my room?"

Her face heated. "Your door was open, and the baby sounded miserable. I'm sorry. I suppose I should've stayed in the hall and called you."

"Nonsense. You did the right thing. I know how loud Gopher can scream. If he didn't wake me, I'm sure you couldn't have."

"Well, it wasn't that he was loud, but his whimpering was pitiful, as if he were in extreme pain. It broke my heart to hear him." She slid the eggs from the iron skillet onto a platter and took the biscuits from the oven.

Cass walked over to the foot of the stairs and yelled, "Breakfast! Come get it while it's hot."

Gazelle came bounding down the stairs with Gander close behind.

Rebekah handed a tray of eggs, grits, ham, milk and a jelly biscuit to Cass. "Would you mind taking this to Goose? Tell her I'll be up shortly to check on her."

"Of course. Kids wash up. I'll be down as soon as I give this to your sister."

His thoughts ran in all sorts of crazy directions. What if he had never sent her away? It was the what-ifs that terrified him. How many times had he done a sketch based on the dangers of vain imaginations? And now, he found himself doing the very thing he preached against. He stopped in the hallway and prayed, "Oh, Father, please create in me a clean heart and renew a right spirit within me, because I don't feel so clean. Lately, I unwittingly find my thoughts propelling me to places and scenarios I have no business going, yet I find myself wanting to stay there instead of shutting out the vain thoughts."

"Father? Are you out there?"

Goose's sweet, angelic voice quickly changed his mood. He walked into her room and was happy to see a smile on his little Goosey Girl's face. "How are you feeling, sweetpea?"

"Better. Guess what? Rebekah made me not itch."

He smiled. "That's good. She's cooked you a nice big

breakfast so try to eat everything, and I'll be back up to get your tray when we finish eating downstairs."

She sat straight up in bed. "I'm hungry. This looks good."

Cass hurried back down to the kitchen, to find Gazelle, Gander and Rebekah seated at the table. He rolled his eyes. "Where's Goat?"

Gazelle shrugged. "I suppose he's still asleep."

Cass stood at the stairs and yelled. "Jonathan Eli Marlowe, wash your hands and get to the table, immediately. I don't want to have to call you again."

Gazelle looked at Rebekah and giggled. "Goat's in big trouble. Anytime Father uses our given name, we know he's not fooling."

After several moments, Cass stomped up the stairs, calling Goat's name. He opened the door and stormed in his son's room. "Goat, I said get out of that—" He didn't want to believe it. He jerked back the covers, but Goat was gone. On top of his pillow was a note. *"I'm tired of the lies. Don't try to find me. You don't care about me so let me be."*

"Gazelle!" He shouted. "Where's your brother?"

She shoved away from the table, ran toward the stairwell and met her father on his way down. "Isn't he in his room?"

"No."

Rebekah wanted to say something to calm his fears, but she had no words.

Cass placed both hands on the back of his head and groaned.

"He was fine when I left. What happened here, yesterday to make him want to leave?"

Gazelle's eyes watered. "Nothing. After he came home from school, I left him in care of the little ones while I went to find Miss Daisy."

"Was he upset when you returned? Maybe angry because you said you'd be back early, and you were late?"

"No. I know he was hoping I'd get home in time for him to play ball with his friends, but he didn't seem upset when Rebekah and I got here."

"Then, that must be it. He must've been angry with you for bringing Rebekah back. I suppose he thought it might upset me."

"No, Father. He was glad to see her."

Rebekah said, "I agree with Gazelle. He wasn't angry. In fact, he tried hard to please me. He made the oatmeal paste for Goose's chicken pox and seemed pleased that I called on him to help."

Gander, listening to the conversation while still sitting at the table, reached for another biscuit. "Father, I helped, too. Didn't I, Gazelle?"

When no one responded to him, he said it a little louder. "I did, didn't I Gazelle? Didn't I help?"

After his third try, he slammed the biscuit on his plate and ran out the door, crying.

Cass threw up his arms. "Now, what's *his* problem." He opened the front door and found Gander sitting up in the sycamore tree, boo-hooing. "What's wrong, son?"

"Nobody listens to me."

"Gander, I'm sorry, if I ignored you, but Goat is missing and I'm worried. As soon as I find your brother, I promise to sit down and listen to anything you want to tell me. Is that a deal?"

He snubbed and nodded. "Deal."

Cass went to the barn and was glad to see the mule and Patches. *He couldn't have gone far.* But after searching until sundown, he went back to the house and told Rebekah he was going into town to ask the sheriff to get up a posse.

The sheriff pretended to be sympathetic, but Cass saw through his fake compassion. "I'm telling you Fletcher, he's lost somewhere in those woods. I've searched all day and I can't find him."

"Cass, we have these kinds of calls all the time. All teenagers run away at some point in their lives, but they always come back when they get hungry."

"Are you saying you're not going to get a posse to help me?"

He glanced up at the sky. "I tell you what I'll do. If Goat isn't home by tomorrow, I'll talk to some of the fellows and see who might be willing to help you comb the woods, but I doubt seriously, it'll come to that."

Cass slammed the door as he went out, then ran across the street to the newspaper office.

The editor met him at the door. "Aft'noon, preacher. What can I do for you?"

"Hank, my boy's missing and I'm scared. I need your help. I'm afraid he's lost in the woods and there are too many acres for me to find him by myself."

He pulled off his cap and ran his fingers through his hair. "Well, with a spread like yours, it'd be hard for a grown man to find his way out. Have you talked to Fletcher? Maybe he could organize a posse."

"He's about as useful as a blind mule."

"I'm getting the print set for tomorrow's edition, now. Why don't I put a notice in the paper and encourage all who can, to help with the search? Since your land isn't confined to one county, I'm sure there are men over around Fruitdale who would be willing to start in that direction."

Cass extended his hand. "Thanks, Hank. I appreciate it."

"No problem. I had some dead space, anyway. Not a lot going on since those hoodlums from up around McIntosh were jailed. I've thought of slipping them a key, just so I'd have something to write about." He let out a loud guffaw, though Cass was in no mood for jokes.

CHAPTER 26

Cass hoped by the time he got home, he'd find Goat waiting there, though his feelings of how he'd handle the situation rocked back and forth. If he should find him at the house, would he hug him or punish him? At the present, he wanted to do both. Why would the kid pull such a thoughtless stunt, especially at a time like this? *Gopher is not well, Goose is still sick with the chicken pox and Miss Daisy won't likely be coming back. I have no idea how Rebekah will react when she finds out I didn't do what I promised. Didn't I have enough on my plate, Lord, without all this?*

Funny how his own sermons always came back to convict him. *"And the Lord said, Simon, Simon, behold, Satan hath desired to have you, that he may sift you like wheat. Luke 22:31."* How many times had he preached that sermon? Now, he felt as if he were the one Satan was putting through the sifter.

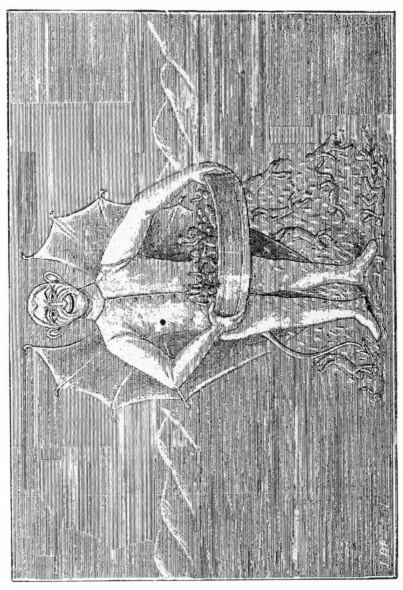

The Devil's Sifter

Rebekah had supper on the table, but being sick with worry, Cass couldn't eat. He said, "How's Goose?"

Rebekah smiled. "She's on the mend but becoming a bit ornery. She feels too bad to play, but she's tired of being sick. Cass, I'm concerned about Gopher. Have you noticed his neck?"

"Are you referring to the bruise?"

"Yes."

"I don't think it's anything to be alarmed about. I recall one of the kids saying Goose tried to lift him from his crib while I was away and dropped him, but that he was alright. I suppose the bruise was caused from the fall." Cass rubbed his temple. "It's Goat that has me worried. He's out there in those woods somewhere, hurting, and I don't know how to help him."

Gazelle said, "Father, it's not as if Goat won't know what to do, even if he has lost his way. No one is more at home in the outdoors. He's forever wanting to point out edible plants when we go berry picking. Even if he's lost, I'm sure he's already made himself a comfortable place to spend the night. You taught him to be a survivor."

Everything she said was right. His boy could've taught Davy Crockett a thing or two about wilderness survival. But Cass wasn't as concerned for Goat's safety as he was frightfully worried about his reason for wanting to leave home. *Lies? When did I ever lie to you, Goat?* He pulled the note from his shirt pocket and read it again, although he had it memorized. Perhaps if he kept looking at it, something would jump out—something he might have said earlier that Goat misunderstood. "I'm tired of the lies. Don't try to find me. You don't care about me so let me be." *What could I have possibly said to make you think I don't care about you? Oh, son. If you only knew how much I love you. Please, don't do this to me.*

After the children were in bed, Cass helped Rebekah clean the kitchen, then they walked out to the porch and sat on the swing.

She said, "Cass, I need to go back to my apartment before daylight, but I don't have a way to get there. I hate to ask, but do you think you might drive me there, tonight?"

He clenched his eyes tight and blew out a lungful of air. "You wanna go?" He bolted out of the swing. "No problem. Everything here is hunky-dory. Get in the car, I'll take you. I asked the Lord tonight what else could go wrong. I think He just answered."

"You're angry."

He walked over and propped against a porch column. "I'm sorry I lashed out. I'm not angry at you, Rebekah. I'm angry at myself. My son has run away because I've led him to believe he's not important in my life. I'm at my wit's end." He turned and walked back to the swing and extended his hand. "Come on. I'll take you back, now. I don't blame you for wanting to go. You've worked hard and I know you're exhausted."

"No, it's not that." She reached for his hand, but instead of rising, she tugged for him to join her in the swing. "Please, sit back down and let's talk."

Their gaze locked and he stood, unmoving holding her hand There was so much he wanted to say to her, but there was no starting place. He eased down beside her.

"Cass, believe me, it's not that I want to leave. I wish I could stay."

"Then, why can't you?"

"Are you serious? Don't you understand what people will accuse you of, when they learn I'm staying here? Your reputation would be ruined, and you'd never have an opportunity to preach again. I can't allow it. Men will be gathering here in the morning by sunup, and I need to be gone. Gazelle is very responsible, and I have every confidence that she can take charge of the household while you're with the search party."

He leaned forward in the swing, then speaking so low, she could barely hear, he said, "Are you finished?"

She pressed her lips together and nodded.

"Fine. Because I have something to tell you. Rebekah—" He took a long pause, then reached for her hand. "Let them talk. We're still married."

Her jaw dropped. "What?" Then catching her breath, she shook her head. "No. You had the marriage annulled. You told me you did."

"No. I never said I did. I said I was going to."

She drew back her hand and placed it in her lap. "Are you saying you lied to me? But why?"

"It wasn't a lie. Well, not intentionally, anyway. I did plan to get it annulled, and I know this is going to sound like an excuse, but things here got so crazy, I let it slip my mind. Then when I remembered, weeks had passed and I knew in that length of time, the judge would require you to be there to confirm that the marriage had not been consummated."

Rebekah sat in silence for several minutes, while Cass waited nervously, wondering what she'd say when she learned the rest of the sordid story.

"Cass, I may be making a fool of myself, but I'm getting conflicting signals from you, and I have to ask: Do you love me?"

His chin trembled. "More than I thought possible to love anyone."

"Do you still want an annulment?"

"No. Do you?"

A crooked little smile lit up her face. "That's good, because I love you, too. I know you'll be busy in the morning looking for Goat, and I wouldn't have it any other way. But as soon as he's back home, I need you to go to the Escatawpa News and have them post a marriage announcement, giving the date we married. That way, anyone who sees me here in the morning, will read of the announcement in the paper, which should squelch all rumors. Will you do that?"

When he was slow to answer, she bit her lip. "I see. You don't want an annulment, but you also don't want folks to know you married a nobody like me."

He stiffened and placed his hands on her shoulders. "Oh,

sweetheart, that is just not true. I'd love for the world to know I'm married to the sweetest, most beautiful, most compassionate woman on the planet. But there's another complication and I don't know how to tell you."

"Figure it out, Cass. We can have no more secrets."

He nodded. "You're right. I don't want secrets." He leaned his head back and closed his eyes, unable to look at her while he bumbled through an explanation that he wished he didn't have to give.

"Honey, my wife . . . that is . . . Amelia is not dead."

"What did you say? Because it sounded as if you said Amelia is not dead. Why would you say that, Cass?" Her lip curled upward. "Unless, of course, you're now trying to finagle out of announcing our marriage?"

"That's not true."

"I know it's not true. I'm aware you were teasing about Amelia, but sweetheart that isn't something to joke about."

"No, you misunderstood. I meant it's not true that I would want to finagle out of announcing the marriage. But it *is* true that Amelia is not dead."

Her smile faded. "Cass, I think the stress of the past week has been too much for you to handle. You're not making sense. Your former wife drowned shortly after Gopher was born. No matter how much you miss her, you have to accept that she won't be back."

He sighed. "If only I could believe that."

She laid her head on his shoulder. "Oh, my sweet Cass, you must believe it. I know you must've loved her very much, but you can't live in denial. Amelia is gone. I'll never be able to take her place with you or the children, but I pray you will all love me for who I am."

His eyes moistened. He had to make her understand. "Rebekah, I, along with everyone else in the region believed she drowned. Why wouldn't we? She told Bertha Baston she was going on a boat ride and picnic with an old friend. Naturally, if you want something to get out quickly, you don't put it in the paper—you tell Bertha. When Amelia failed to return, and two straw hats were found in the water, and the empty boat drifted down to shore, what other possible explanation could have occurred?"

Rebekah's eyes darkened. "I'm thinking the same thing."

"Honey, listen to what I'm saying. Amelia faked her death."

"Oh, Cass." She reached over and rubbed the back of her hand across his cheek. "You poor darling. I'm afraid you're having a breakdown. I know you're terribly worried about Goat, but in my heart, I know he's okay. After he comes home, I insist that you see Doc Brunson."

"You have to believe me, Rebekah. Amelia. Is. Not. Dead."

"Okay, calm down and let's talk about it. If she isn't dead, when did you learn that she's still alive?"

"I can't recall the date, it would be on the letter. I suppose it was about a month or so after you left."

"Letter? Are you saying she wrote you to let you know she

was still alive?"

"Yes." He ran his fingers through his hair.

"Cass, can't you see this doesn't make sense?"

"I never said it did. But it's true."

"Why would she go to the trouble to fake her death, then write to you to let you know it was a farce?"

He leaned forward with his elbows planted on his knees and his hands cupped around his face. "Because she needed a divorce."

"Did you give it to her?"

"Yes."

"Then you're saying you were married to her when you married me?"

"Rebekah, please let me finish before you start asking questions. When I'm done, if you don't believe me, then we won't discuss it further. I'll take you back to your apartment if that's what you choose to do."

"Alright, Cass. I'm listening."

"Rebekah, Amelia and I married young. My father was a wealthy planter and he was against the marriage from the beginning, but whatever Amelia set her mind on, she usually got. I thought I loved her, but I didn't know what love was until the day I met you."

Her palm shot up. "Stop. Don't try to sweet talk me. I'm only interested in hearing about your dead wife who isn't dead and the divorce you didn't get until after we were married. I think I have that much right."

The front door opened, and Goose walked out on the porch in her nightgown, whining. "I'm itching and I can't sleep."

Cass threw up his hands. "Goose, go back to bed and I'll be in a little later to give you a dose of aspirin."

Rebekah shot a sharp glance at Cass, rose and took Goose by the hand. "Come on, sweetie, I'll go rub you down. I'm sorry you're itching." She opened the screen door, then turned to face Cass. "Goodnight."

"You aren't coming back?"

"I think we've said enough for one night. I need to let some of this sink in."

Rebekah was cooking breakfast at four-thirty the following morning when Cass walked into the kitchen.

"You're up early." He walked over and stood beside her. "Rebekah, about last night."

"Not now, Cass. The men will be gathering here shortly."

Before he could say anything, Gopher let out a blood-curdling scream and Cass ran to the bedroom, picked him up and took him to the kitchen.

Rebekah wiped her hands on a dish rag and held out her arms. "Hand him to me and I'll go change him. Your breakfast is ready."

Minutes later, she walked back into the kitchen with Gopher's head nuzzled under her chin. She tried to spoon-feed him soft-scrambled eggs, but he tightened his lips and turned his head. "Cass, I know you don't want to hear this, but when I changed his diaper, what I saw disturbed me. If I was a mother, I could blame what I'm feeling on a mother's instinct, but I'm not and I'm not a medical professional, but I'm telling you, this baby needs help."

"I agree, he's a sickly child, but I've taken him to the nation's best doctors, and they assured me if there was a need to be alarmed, they would let me know. I haven't heard a word, so I assume whatever is ailing him is not serious and hopefully he'll outgrow it."

Her teeth made a grinding noise. "That is not good enough. How can he outgrow anything if he isn't getting nourishment?" Tears flowed from her eyes. "I can't get him to eat."

"Hey, now who's the one having a breakdown?"

She wiped her eyes with the back of her hand. "I'm sorry. I don't know why I cry so easily, now. I never have before." She stopped and cocked her head, slightly. "I think I heard cars driving up. They're here. Go on outside."

"I hate to leave you like this. Why don't I wake Gazelle and let her take Gopher and you go lie back down and try to sleep? You've been overdoing it."

She jerked away when he rested his hand upon her shoulder. "I'm fine. Go!"

CHAPTER 27

Rebekah jiggled Gopher in her arms, while walking the floor. She ambled over to the parlor window and watched as hordes of men gathered around Cass for directions. Within minutes, they had all dispersed.

Gazelle and the twins came down for breakfast. It was good to see Goose feeling better, although the usual breakfast chatter was missing. Finally, Gander said, "It's too quiet without Goat. I wonder where he went?"

Rebekah poured three glasses of milk. "I don't know, sweetheart, but your Father will find him."

After breakfast, Gazelle was helping Rebekah with the dishes when the phone rang.

"Reverend Marlowe's residence, Gazelle speaking."

"Yes, this is Dr. Callahan and I'm looking for Reverend Castle Marlowe. Is he in?"

"No, sir. I'm his daughter. Can I take a message?"

"No, I need to speak to him directly. Where can I reach him?"

"I'm afraid he can't be reached."

"Well if you should hear from him, please tell him it's vital that he contact me. I'll be at the Mobile Infirmary."

Her lip trembled. "It's about my little brother, isn't it? What's wrong with him?"

"I'm sorry, but I can't divulge that information to anyone but the child's father—" There was a brief pause. "Is the child's mother there?"

Gazelle bit her lip before answering. "Yessir, I'll get her." She placed her hand over the phone's receiver and whispered to Rebekah, "I had to tell a tiny fib. It's Gopher's doctor and he says it's urgent information, but he'll only give it to Gopher's parents. I sorta said you were his mother."

Rebekah took the phone. "Hello."

"Hello, ma'am. Dr. Callahan here. Are you the Reverend Marlowe's wife?"

She sucked in a heavy breath, then exhaled. "Yes. Yes, I am his wife."

"Well, I'll make this brief, I need little Enoch here by ten o'clock tomorrow morning. We will be set up by then and need both you and your husband here, also, for blood testing."

"For *what*?"

"Ma'am, the tests we took when your husband brought him to the Infirmary, have come back and Dr. Biggs and I agree your little boy is losing blood. In order to save his life, we need to do a blood transfusion as soon as possible."

"What is blood-testing?"

"I don't have time to explain the mechanics, Mrs. Marlowe, but not everyone has the same type blood. You and your husband both may share the same type as your little boy, or it could be only one of you, but the blood type of the donor must match the blood type of the recipient. I'll expect you promptly at ten o'clock, tomorrow. I'm sure you have many questions, so feel free to ask and I'll do my best to answer your concerns at that time."

"Thank you, doctor, but I prefer you have this conversation with . . . Enoch's father. Is there a number where he can reach you tonight?" After she wrote down the number, she held the phone in her hand for several seconds after he had hung up.

Gazelle stood with hands clasped beneath her chin. "What did he say? What did the doctor say was wrong with Gopher?"

Rebekah sat the phone back on the cradle. "He wants Gopher to have a blood transfusion. I've never heard of such."

"We studied about it in Science. But I don't want him to go through that. He could die."

"Well, honey, I don't like the sound of it, either, but I'm sure your Father will make the right decision."

Rebekah reflected on her response when the doctor asked if she was Cass's wife. Maybe she lied. Maybe she didn't. She wasn't sure of anything, anymore.

Gazelle carried Gopher around on her hip every waking minute and Rebekah tried to stay busy to keep from thinking about all that was going on. Would Gopher survive a blood transfusion? What if the fellows couldn't find Goat? Did he take food with him? She knew Cass believed Amelia wasn't dead, but the idea was ludicrous. Was he under so much stress, he had begun to imagine things? If he was imagining something that bizarre, then perhaps he really did get the annulment, but his mind is playing tricks. Yet, if it were true, and he divorced Amelia *after* they were married, where did that leave her? Would the courts say he was a bigamist? Was she really married, or not?

Rebekah was hanging a load of wash on the line, when a car pulled up in the yard and a stranger got out. "Ma'am, are you the lady of the house?"

She looked down at the basket of wet clothes and smiled. "I suppose I am. What do you need?"

"I'm Josephus Anders from the Escatawpa News. I came by to see if the boy has been found."

"No, but I'm sure he will be. There's a search party out looking for him now."

She glanced over at the Sycamore tree, just in time to see Gander's foot slip. She yelled, "Be careful, honey. I think you've climbed high enough."

The reporter appeared agitated. "Ma'am, have you had any leads?"

"What kind of leads?"

"It's a known fact that Castle Marlowe is a very wealthy man. Have you considered the possibility the boy could've been kidnapped?"

"No, but if you'll excuse me, I have work to do."

She reached down in the basket, pulled out a sheet and hung it on the line to dry.

The reporter lumbered back to his car and drove off.

Cass came back home long after dark. The children were all in bed and Rebekah waited on the porch. She stood when she saw him walking from the woods on the east side of the house.

"You couldn't find him?"

He shook his head and stumbled up the steps. "I've walked and yelled for hours, but if he heard me, he chose not to let me find him. The fellows all gave up about sundown. I could tell they were sympathetic, but they think he's hiding and will come home when he gets hungry."

"What do you think?"

"I think I've hurt him, deeply. I haven't been much of a father or I would know what this is all about. I've racked my brain for answers."

"Come on inside and eat a bite. I know you must be hungry."

"I haven't had time to think about eating, but I suppose I should eat something."

"I recall you saying you like fried ham, buttered biscuits and syrup for supper, so it's on the stove."

"That does sound good."

Gazelle came barreling down the stairs. "I heard you talking.

Father, did you find Goat?"

"No, sweetheart, but I'm not giving up. I'll start again tomorrow. It got too dark to find my way through the woods."

Cass said, "Gazelle, think hard. Can you recall Goat ever mentioning anything about me lying to him?"

Her nose crinkled. "You? Lying. No sir, why would you ask?"

He pulled out the note and handed to her.

Her eyes bulged. "I have no idea what he meant. It seems strange, because right before we went to bed, we were playing cards together, and he seemed fine."

"What did you talk about?"

She lifted a shoulder. "I don't remember. Nothing important."

"Like what? Maybe it didn't seem important to you at the time, but there could be a clue lurking in your conversation. Maybe he said something like, 'Father promised to take me fishing, but he lied?'"

She shook her head. "No sir. He was in fine spirits all day. We talked that afternoon, right before I left to go find Miss Daisy, and he was quite happy, so it seems really odd that he'd up and run away in the middle of the night."

"Do you know why he appeared to be in good spirits?"

"Yessir. It was because Katie invited him to the picnic. He's had a crush on her, forever. He really wanted to go, even after I told him he'd have to dress up. You know how he hates to wear a coat and tie. He was worried his coat wouldn't fit but I suggested he try on yours."

"Try to remember his exact words."

Gazelle went over the conversation with her Father.

He sighed. "I don't get it. If he was looking forward to the picnic, why would he decide to run away?"

Rebekah said, "Now, I understand why your coat was on the floor. I thought it odd, since it wasn't like you to throw it down."

Cass squinted. "What?"

"Gazelle said she suggested your coat might fit him. I suppose he tried it on, but instead of hanging it up, he threw it on the floor."

"Stay put. I need to check on something." Cass jumped up and ran down the hall to his room. He pulled his black jacket from his closet and thrust his hand in the pocket. His heart pounded, even before he pulled his hand out. He could feel crumpled paper, evidence that Goat had read the letter. Cass distinctly remembered folding it. Now, the pieces fit. Not wanting to break Gazelle's heart by revealing her mother's scam, he hung the jacket up, with the letter still in the pocket.

He trudged back to the kitchen.

Rebekah said, "Oh, I almost forgot. Cass, Dr. Callahan from Mobile called earlier and asked to have you call him."

"Did he mention why?"

"He wants to talk with you about a treatment for Gopher." She didn't have the heart to tell him. "His number is written on the chalkboard above the phone."

Gazelle blurted. "They want to do a blood transfusion. You

won't allow it, will you, Father? Gopher is too young. I'm afraid it could kill him."

"Hold on, Gazelle." His gaze locked with Rebekah's. "A blood transfusion? That's what he said?"

"Yes. Call him and he'll explain."

Cass rubbed his hands across his face and shouted. "Where are you, Lord? This is more than I can handle." He ambled over, picked up the phone, then dropped it, and like a limp dishrag he crumpled to the floor, sobbing.

Seeing her father in agony, Gazelle burst into tears and ran up to her room.

Rebekah pumped water onto a cloth, knelt beside him and gently washed his face with cold water.

His lip quivered. "I suppose you think I'm weak. Men aren't supposed to cry."

She suddenly forgot why she was angry with him. "You've had a lot to bear. I'm so sorry, Cass. I wish there was something I could do to ease the pain."

"I think I'm ready to make that call now." He stood and called the number on the blackboard. The doctor was adamant that Gopher was in need of a blood transfusion and very thorough in his explanation of what would take place. The doctor's last words played over and over in Cass's head, like a scratched Victrola record, when he said, "I'm hoping I'm wrong, but if I'm right, he won't have a chance without a transfusion. You're his father. It'll be your call."

When he hung up, he said, "What am I gonna do, Rebekah? How can I leave home, not knowing where Goat is? But how can I stay, when according to the doctor, if I don't get the transfusion for Gopher, he'll die."

"Cass, you have to go and do what you can to save Gopher. Goat may be angry, but he was in no danger of losing his life when he left, and I don't believe that has changed. He's a smart boy. When he has time to think about whatever he's dealing with, I'm sure he'll come home."

"I wish I could be as confident."

"I'll pack a bag for you and Gopher, and you can be ready to leave after breakfast in the morning."

"Thank you. Rebekah . . . are you still angry that I didn't tell you about the letter, sooner?"

"Please, Cass. This is not the time. We'll deal with our problems later. At the present, we have two—" She gasped. Why did she say 'we?' She started over. "At the present, you have two sons who need your full attention."

"You're right. I couldn't have made it this far without you, Rebekah. Thank you."

Friday morning, Rebekah cooked breakfast, bathed and dressed Gopher, and had a lunch packed for Cass to take on the trip. Gazelle, Gander and Goose were up early to see their father and baby brother off.

Rebekah walked him to the car. "We'll be praying, Cass." She watched as he drove away and wondered if she'd ever see her sweet little Gopher again. Fighting back the tears, she had to stay strong for the sake of the children.

The search party, made up of men from the community gathered together in the front yard. She watched as one fellow drew a map in the dirt. The men all circled around it, then divided up, with each team agreeing to take a section of land in an effort to find Goat.

Rebekah tried to stay busy every minute to keep her mind from going down a depressing path. Around eight-thirty, Gazelle was in her room reading and the twins were playing marbles in the back yard. She was on the porch darning Cass's socks when she saw an automobile coming down the road. When it whipped up in front of the house, she laid her knitting on the swing and walked to the edge of the porch. A well-dressed lady stepped out of the car.

Rebekah assumed she was lost. "Are you looking for someone?"

The woman ignored her question and kept walking toward her. There was something about her that looked familiar, but she couldn't recall where she might have seen her.

"Where's Cass?"

It wasn't so much the question as the arrogant attitude that caused Rebekah to bristle. "He isn't here."

"When do you expect him back?"

"I'm not sure. Can I help you?"

"No, I'll wait for him."

The woman's gaze trailed from the top of Rebekah's head to the bottom of her feet. "I suppose you're the nanny?"

Rebekah said, "My name is Rebekah. And you are—?"

"Never mind who I am. Where are the children?"

Rebekah's heart raced, when she realized why the woman looked familiar. *The painting above the mantle. It's her.* She swallowed hard. "Cass isn't here."

"You said that already." The woman opened the front door and went into the house.

Rebekah followed after her. "I know who you are."

"You know, yet you don't seem shocked to see me. How could that be?"

"Please go and come back when Cass is here."

Her brow lifted. "Excuse me, young lady, but I don't think it's appropriate for you to be calling my husband by his given name."

"Why are you here?"

"I read in the paper that my oldest son is missing. I want to be here when he's found."

"Please, Mrs.—"

"The name's Marlowe, hon. Mrs. Castle Marlowe."

CHAPTER 28

Gazelle was in her room when she heard voices downstairs, one which sounded eerily like her deceased mother's. She tiptoed down the hall and leaned over the banister, hoping to see who was talking to Rebekah.

Assuming it too good to be true, it took her several moments to realize it wasn't her imagination. Squealing, she ran down the stairs with tears flowing from her eyes. "Mother, you're alive. I can't believe it's really you. Where have you been? What happened?"

Amelia threw her arms around her daughter and planted kisses on the side of her face. "Oh, sweetheart, how you've grown. And what a beautiful young lady, you are. Let me look you over." She held her at arm's length, and said, "Why, I feel as if I'm looking in a mirror. You're my spitting image. I'm sure that pleases your father. Before you were born, he said he hoped if we had a little girl she would look exactly like me. I do believe he got his wish." She reached up and ran her finger over a tear falling from

Gazelle's eyes. "This is no time for tears, sweetheart."

"Oh, Mother, they're happy tears. I can't believe it's you. We all thought you were dead. Where have you been?"

"Sugar, it's a long story, but the short version is a friend of mine from out of town came to visit and we went for a boat ride. We were kidnapped and taken to New Orleans. I finally managed to escape and I could hardly wait to get back home to my wonderful husband and children. Did you miss me a lot?"

"Oh, we missed you so much." Gazelle wrapped her arms around her mother's waist. "I'm so sorry you were kidnapped, but at least we have you back now. What happened to your friend?"

Rebekah waited—eager to hear the answer.

"I don't know, sweetheart. There were two men who kidnapped us. One took me with him and the other one took my friend. I haven't seen her since that day."

"Oh, Mother, that is so dreadful. Goose and Gander are playing out back. I'm sure they'll be excited to see you."

"And I, them, sweetheart. You children—and your father, of course—were the only thing that kept me going. I was determined that someway, somehow, I'd find my way back to you."

Gazelle and Amelia walked down the hall and out the back door. Rebekah peered out the window at the twins when they looked up and realized it was their mother. Yet, their greeting was not as warm and welcoming as Gazelle's had been.

Amelia knelt down and held out her arms, but Goose and Gander kept their distance. "Come here, sweetie. Don't you remember me? I'm your mother."

Goose said, "I know who you are."

Gander completely ignored her. "It's your turn to shoot, Goose."

Gazelle seemed embarrassed for her mother and made excuses for the twins' behavior. "I can hardly wait for Father to return. Boy, will he be surprised to find you here."

She smiled. "Yes, I'm you're right."

"Mother, you haven't asked about Gopher."

"Who?" She popped her hand over her mouth. "Oh, the baby. I assume that's the nickname your father gave Enoch. If he's sleeping, we won't wake him."

"Gopher has been really sick for a long time. Father has taken him to the hospital in Mobile and he's going to have a blood transfusion. That is, if Father's blood is a match."

Rebekah hoped it was her imagination, but it looked as if Amelia were pleased to hear the grim report.

Amelia said, "When did they leave?"

"This morning. He's supposed to meet with the doctor at ten o'clock."

"Honey, that breaks my heart. I hate to rush off, but I want to go see my darling Enoch. You understand, don't you?"

"Sure, Mother. I can't wait for Father to discover you're alive."

"You think he'll be pleased, do you?"

"Of course, he will. You know how much he loved you."

The words cut through Rebekah's heart as if someone had stabbed her and twisted the knife.

Amelia picked up the tail of her skirt and hurried toward the front of the house to her car. Gazelle ran behind her, but her mother jumped in the car, cranked it and waved out the window of her fancy automobile as she drove away.

Gander came in the house. "Where did that woman go?"

Gazelle said, "She's not *that woman*. She's your mother."

"My mother's dead. She drowned in the river."

"No. That's what we thought. But she's alive."

"I don't care. I don't like her."

"Gander! That's an awful thing to say. She loves us very much."

Goose said, "Then why did she go away again?"

"She didn't know about Gopher and when I told her he was in the hospital, she was in a hurry to see him. Mother loves all of us children."

Goose said, "Does she love Father, too?"

"That's a silly question. He's her husband. Of course, she loves him." As soon as the words escaped her lips, the strange questions Goat asked the day before he left, flashed through her mind.

"Do you ever wish Mother and Father were still married? Do you think they loved each other? Just because two people marry, it's no sign they're in love. I wonder if they were in love when they married. I wonder if they were ever in love."

But it was not so much the questions that troubled her, as the story he told later, when he said, *"I didn't think much about it when it happened, but I remember one time I was fishing down at the river. About five-hundred feet from the dock, there's a spot where I've been catching a lot of crappy. I hardly ever throw a hook in there that I don't pull up a fish. Nobody knows about it but me. It's an eddy at the bend of the river, hidden by a clomp of reeds, so even when a boat passes, they don't see me.*

So one day, I go down there and I see Mother down there talking to a man wearing fancy white clothes, and he had a big, fine boat docked at our ramp."

Her pulse raced. Goat must've seen the kidnapper. She closed her eyes, wanting to remember the entire conversation. He said Mother told him the man was a stranger, asking directions…but then Goat made the comment that it didn't bother him at the time, but after thinking about it, he felt a man with such a fine boat would likely know exactly where he was. He didn't say it in so many words, but I think he was trying to tell me he thought Mother was lying.

"They were laughing and carrying on like ol' buddies, until they saw me. Gazelle, I don't think he was a stranger. And you know something else? The next day, Mother went missing. Don't you think that's odd?"

She recalled how upset he was that she accused him of subconsciously wanting to be angry with Mother for dying and leaving them.

He accused Gazelle of not listening to what he was trying to tell her. *He was right and I was wrong. I wasn't listening.* She tried to dismiss the thoughts filling her head. *I think I know now what Goat was getting at, but he was wrong. She wasn't having a rendezvous. The man was a kidnapper.* But if he was the kidnapper, where was her Mother's friend?

Rebekah walked outside and sat down on the porch steps beside Gazelle. "Are you okay?"

"Sure. Why wouldn't I be? My mother's alive."

"Yes, she is."

"She's gone to be with Father and Gopher."

"I heard."

"Do you think he'll be happy to see her?"

Rebekah reached for her hand. "I don't know. Can you think of a reason he wouldn't be thrilled to see his wife—the mother of his children—whom he believed for months to be dead?"

The telephone rang before Gazelle had a chance to answer. She jumped up. "I'll get it." A couple of minutes later, she yelled, "Rebekah, it's Father and he wants to speak to you."

Rebekah answered and could hear the tension in his voice.

"Have they located Goat?"

"No, but they haven't stopped looking. How are things there?"

"We're coming home."

Her heart pounded. "Today? Did the doctors decide Gopher doesn't need the transfusion, after all?"

"No. He needs it, but I'm not a match." He broke down on the phone.

"Cass, listen. Don't give up and don't leave. Amelia is on her way there. Maybe, she's a match."

"You've seen Amelia?"

"Yes, and she should be at the hospital shortly."

"Praise the Lord. Not that I care about seeing her, but I'll put up with anything if she can save Gopher." His voice cracked.

****

Rebekah was frying chicken when the phone rang. She grabbed it. "Cass, is that you?"

"Yeah, it's me."

"Tell me what's going on. Have they tested Amelia?"

"No."

"No? When will they do it?"

"They won't. She wouldn't agree to be tested."

"What? That's crazy. Didn't the doctors tell her the consequences?"

"She didn't even see the doctors. When I told her what I needed her to do, she wouldn't agree. She pitched a fit and left the hospital. So, I'll be bringing him back home tonight."

"No. Stay there."

"Why?"

"Because I'm coming. I want to be tested."

"What are the chances, Rebekah? I'm his Father, and I'm no match."

"I don't know, but we have to at least try. I've just finished frying chicken. I'll get Gazelle to finish up the lunch and I'll ride Patches to the depot and be on the next train to Mobile."

"Okay. I'm glad you're coming. Gopher needs you, but I need you, too."

She took Patches to the livery stable, then walked to the depot and bought a ticket. The next train to Mobile was scheduled to leave in thirty-five minutes. It was the longest thirty-five minutes of her life.

When she arrived in Mobile, she was surprised to find Cass waiting for her.

He grabbed her in a hug. "It seems as if I haven't seen you in a month."

"It has been a dreadfully long twenty-four hours, hasn't it?"

"I called to find out what time your train would arrive, and it has felt like time was standing still."

"I'm sorry you had to leave Gopher to come get me. But I want you to promise that as soon as you get me to the hospital, that you'll go home to the children."

"No. That won't happen. I can't leave you and Gopher."

"Don't be ridiculous, Cass. We have three of the nation's best doctors caring for us. I'll be with Gopher. You need to be home when Goat arrives. He'll need you. They all need you. They're frightened and don't need to be left alone."

"You believe he'll come back. Don't you?"

"Of course, I do. But he's a confused young man and needs his father's assurance that whatever he has built up in his head is false. Where's your car? Let's waste no time."

"I'm parked out front. They have Gopher asleep, whether medically induced or he's sleeping a lot on his own, I can't say. He's white as a sheet, Rebekah. If he pulls out of this, it will be a miracle."

"Then let's pray for a miracle."

"Don't think I haven't."

Cass opened her car door, then ran around and slid behind the steering wheel. Rebekah grabbed her hat, when a gust of wind blew through the open window.

"The doctors have informed me that if you do happen to be a match, we should be prepared for you and Gopher to stay at least two weeks at the hospital." He reached across the car seat and took her hand. "Rebekah, I know the unknown must be frightening to you. I understand. Are you sure this is what you want to do?"

"Don't be foolish, Cass. My only thoughts are of Gopher. I'm eager to begin the procedure. Can't you drive faster?"

As he drove, Cass told her Dr. Biggs told of a newborn in 1908 who received a blood transfusion with great success. "I want to believe if a newborn could survive it, our little Gopher can."

Our?

"Yes. If you can save him, he'll have your blood, as well as mine running through his veins. I think that makes him ours, don't you?" He squeezed her hand.

When they arrived at the hospital, he walked Rebekah inside and met briefly with the doctors. She was placed on a gurney and whisked down the hall, while Cass walked beside her, holding her hand.

"Cass, please go. You're needed worse at home than you are here."

"I can't leave you, Rebekah. Doc Brunson called the hospital earlier and said his wife was insisting I stay with you and Gopher at least until the tests come back. Said she'd be happy to go sit with the kids and see they get fed. I've agreed to take her up on her offer."

CHAPTER 29

The test results finally came back, revealing Rebekah was a match. The nurse quickly prepped her as they explained the procedure. When tears filled her eyes, the doctor attempted to calm her, assuming she was afraid.

"I'm not afraid for me, Dr. Biggs. I'm afraid for the baby."

He squeezed her hand. "You're giving your child the only chance he has. You'll always know in your heart that you did all you could to save him."

"But Gopher isn't—"

He placed his hand gently on her forearm. "I know what you're going to say. You want to know if your baby will die. I know how hard it is to ask, but believe it or not, it is almost as difficult for me, when I realize the responsibility that lies in my hands. Mrs. Marlowe, I sincerely wish that I could assure you the transfusion will work, and your little boy could lead a long, healthy life, but I can make no promises. Together, we'll do all we can.

Life and death is in the hands of the Lord."

Although Rebekah coveted assurance, it wasn't what she intended to say before the doctor interrupted. He had erroneously assumed she was Gopher's mother, for whom they'd been waiting. She was trying to tell him Gopher wasn't her child. Did it matter? Her blood matched and that was the only thing that did matter.

She felt a painful sting when the needle pierced her skin and she turned her head to keep from looking at the baby. She was afraid she'd come off the table with the needle in her arm if she were to see him take his last breath. "Please, Lord, please let this work."

Whether she passed out or the doctors gave her something to make her sleep, she didn't know. But the next thing she remembered, Dr. Biggs was leaning over her, saying, "You did good, little Mama."

"It's over?"

He smiled. "It's over."

She looked over at the stretcher beside her and Gopher was gone. "Where's the baby? Is he?" She burst into sobs.

"Hey, he's in ICU being monitored. Everything is running as expected up to now. Time will tell."

She started to sit up.

"Not so fast. I need for you to lie flat until I tell you it's okay to sit up. You're gonna be light-headed and could fall."

"Do you have any aspirin powders? I have a terrific headache."

The nurse was standing nearby. "I'll go get it, doctor."

"How much longer do we have to stay here?"

He smiled. "Don't you like us?"

"I do. You've all been wonderful, but I have obligations and need to get back."

"Mr. Marlowe tells me you have four other children. You look very young to be the mother of five children."

"They aren't all mine." She swallowed hard. *What made me say they aren't all mine? Why didn't I say none of them are mine?*

"Well, I can tell you're a very caring person and the children are blessed to have you in their lives."

The nurse brought in several books for Rebekah to choose from, and she chose one called Wuthering Heights. It helped pass the time until they finally allowed her to ride a wheelchair down the hall to the nursery, where she could look at Goat through a plate glass window. It made her cry, each time she looked at him. So small. So frail. He not only owned her blood, he owned her heart.

Cass is right. He *is* our baby.

****

It was getting dark and Gazelle vowed not to go back to the house until her Father returned and she wasn't sure when that would be. Though she didn't start out with a planned destination, she found herself wandering through the pasture and wound up at her Father's prayer stump. She sat down and buried her face in her hands, hoping the pain would translate into a prayer, but the words wouldn't come. Bitterness filled her heart as she recalled the memorial service they held for her mother, after ending the week-long search for dead bodies. What a sham. Gazelle recalled how her grieving father had placed a lovely tombstone nearby, under the Mulberry tree, as a memorial. She blinked back tears, recalling the agony she felt as she listened to her father that day, sobbing as each child placed a flower at the foot of the monument.

For months after the funeral, she suffered nightmares of her mother drowning, splashing in the river, screaming for help. Gazelle's sympathy was no longer directed toward her mother, since she now blamed her for Goat running away. If she had anywhere to go, she'd run away, too, but she wasn't wilderness savvy the way her brother was. She had no doubt he could live off the wild forever. If only she'd listened to what he was trying to tell her the day before he left, maybe she'd be with him now. He could teach her how to live with nature. Not knowing what else to do, she was almost resigned to going back.

****

Several days after the transfusion, torn between staying at the hospital, being at home with the children, and searching for Goat, Cass gave in to Rebekah's insistence and agreed to go home to check on the children.

When he pulled up in front of the Amelia House, there were several cars parked in front, which he assumed belonged to fellows who continued to search for Goat. His throat tightened when only two children ran to greet him. He picked up Goose and felt Gander grab his other hand. Cass said, "Where's Gazelle?"

Goose said, "She's not here."

"I see that. Where is she?"

"We don't know. She wasn't here at breakfast."

Goat said, "I think she's mad at Mother."

He stopped in his tracks and eased Goose to the ground. Surely, he didn't hear what he thought he heard. "Mad with who?"

Goose said, "Our mother's back. She's come to live with us."

She's here? "Kids, your mother and I have grown-up talk to discuss. Why don't you two stay outside and play, and when we're done, I'll come out and tell you all about Gopher. Deal?"

"Okay, Father." Goose pointed to a board sitting atop concrete blocks. "Look! We've got a new see-saw. Mother made it for us."

"Fine. Go see-saw. I'll be out later to watch."

He hurried inside and heard a commotion in the back of the house. Stomping into the kitchen, he saw Amelia wearing an apron, with her hands in a bowl of flour.

The skin around his eyes tightened. "Where's Mrs. Brunson?"

"I sent her home. Sweet ol' soul was overjoyed to learn I was alive and well and had managed to escape my kidnappers."

"Why did you come back, Amelia?"

"I live here, remember?" She smiled. "My name is on the arch at the end of the road. This is where my children live."

"Amelia, you gave up rights to these children the day you decided to be declared dead. As far as the children and I are concerned, you're still dead. I want you out of my house, immediately."

"Don't be such a hot head, Cass. It doesn't suit you, preacher!" She washed the flour from her hands, walked over and draped her arms around his neck. "We had something very good at one time. Remember? We can have it again."

He prized her arms from his neck. "I said get out, but before you do, I want to know where I can find Gazelle."

She laughed, then walked over, picked up a wet rag and wiped flour from off the pie safe's porcelain countertop. "Cass, she's just trying her reins as a teenager. The dramatics come with the territory."

"I want to know what happened between you two to make her leave."

"I know you want to blame me, Cass, but that little smart-aleck attitude of hers is your fault. You've spoiled her. I would never have put up with that sassy mouth and I've made it understood that I won't allow it now. She's off somewhere blowing off steam. She was never like this before I—"

"Before what, Amelia? Before you died?"

She blew him off with a wave of her hand. "Excuse me, hon, but I need to get the dumplings cut. I'm making your favorite chicken and dumplings for supper. Of course, I could never make them like Aunt Jewel."

"I don't want anything you cook, Amelia."

He went into his room to change clothes and saw her trunk

there. A pair of her shoes were underneath his bed, and a petticoat and couple of fancy dresses hung in his closet. He jerked them down and crammed them into the trunk, then took the trunk and placed it on the porch.

Walking back into the kitchen, he said, "Your clothes are on the porch. If you'll tell me which automobile is yours, I'll put it on the rumble seat."

"Cass, I made a mistake. A huge mistake. I blame it on after-birth blues. Gopher was only a few weeks old and I was going through a time of depression. You can understand, can't you? I felt after five children, I was losing my figure and I needed to prove to myself that I was still desirable."

Cass's jaw flexed, but he let her talk.

"Wyatt and I met on a cruise before you and I married. He was crazy about me, but don't you see? I chose you, darling. I hadn't seen him for years. Then, one day while out shopping we ran into one another. He looked at me as if I were the same sixteen-year-old beauty he once fell in love with, even though I was three months pregnant and had put on weight. I felt frumpy and was flattered that he found me desirable. When he said he now owned The Goldwing Riverboat Casino in New Orleans, he made it sound like such a glamorous lifestyle. Can't you understand? I didn't choose Wyatt over you. I chose glamour over the mundane. Life had become boring, and in my depressed state, I thought I needed the excitement of living on a Riverboat."

"Then go back and live the lifestyle that suits you, Amelia, because you have no place here. We're divorced. Remember?"

"You aren't listening, Cass. The divorce was a mistake. I was despondent and didn't know what I was doing. I've come to my senses and realize that you are all I want. All I've ever really wanted."

"Who are you trying to convince, Amelia? You moved out of our bedroom months before Gopher was born. In fact, as soon as you discovered you were pregnant, I had the feeling you loathed me." He tried hard to ignore the fearsome thought that tried to make its way into his head. Maybe he was naïve, but until now, he had not even considered the sickening possibility. *No, Satan. You're wrong. He's mine.*

"It was hormones, Cass. I've read all about it. But I feel differently, now. That's why I'm moving back into our bedroom."

"No. No, you're not. You're moving out of the house."

"You can't make me. I'll ruin your ministry. I'll tell folks—"

"Tell them what? That you ran off with another man, sent me divorce papers to sign so you could marry your lover, the Riverboat Casino owner?"

"But I didn't marry him."

He chuckled. "Oh, that's good. You simply lived with him for a year, but you didn't marry him." He stormed out of the kitchen, then stopped in the hall, turned and went back and stood in the doorway. "By the way, you can throw the dumplings in the garbage. I'll be taking Goose and Gander to eat at Maude's."

She glared. "I see you have a car, now. I begged and pleaded with you to buy one for over two years, but you wouldn't, just to antagonize me."

"I had no objections to a car, but I wouldn't get one at the time because of your reasoning. You said you wanted one because people of means were riding cars. You felt riding in a buggy made us look like simple folk."

"It was true, and you know it."

"Well, you convinced me, and since I happen to like simple folk, it didn't seem like such a terrible thing to look like one. I've never liked putting on airs."

"But you bought one after I left."

"Yep. I needed a quicker way to travel the circuit so I could have a speedier way to return home to my children, since their Mother deserted them for her lover."

She produced a few soft sobs and said, "I told you I wasn't thinking straight. I love you, and you only, Cass Marlowe. I've heard you preach that God is a God of second chances. Can't you be?"

"Turn off the tear faucet, Amelia. It used to work. No more. I'll expect you to be gone when I return."

CHAPTER 30

Cass stomped down the hall and rushed out the front door. He picked up an axe, got into his car and rode to the end of the dirt road leading to the house.

With a few good swings of the axe the sign bearing the name Amelia House, came tumbling to the ground. By the time he arrived back at the house, the sun was going down and men were returning from the woods. They were all concerned about Gopher's condition and wanted to assure Cass that their prayers hadn't stopped, and neither would the search party. Not until Goat was found and little Gopher was back home.

"I thank you fellows. I know you've taken time away from your farms to look for my son and I appreciate it. Beginning at daybreak, I'll be able to search on my own, since I plan to be here for quite a while. Unless—" He choked up. "Unless my baby doesn't pull through the procedure, at which time I'll go bring him back home."

Roscoe Jones patted him on the shoulder. "Oh, Lawdy. Makes

me shiver just to think about it, preacher, although I reckon it's weighin' on all of us. I saw the little fellow just before you took him off, and I Suwannee, he looked like his next breath could be his last. But me and the missus are praying every day that it don't come to that. We sho' are. We've lost two young'un's and there ain't nothing in this world harder than burying one of your own."

Cass knew he meant well but tried to change the subject. "Roscoe, I rode by your place and it looked like you've cleared some land."

"Yeah, our oldest boy, Tullis, is getting married and him and his bride gonna build 'em a little house nearby. He says they want to help take care of his mama. She's been doing poorly for quite a spell."

"I'm sorry to hear that. Maebelle is a good woman."

"Yessir, you right about that. Yesterday, when I started on the search, I saw your wife's tombstone under the Mulberry tree. Made me tear up, just thinking about yo' little ol' young'uns, and wondering what they might be going through. You reckon that's why Goat ran away? Scares the daylights out of me, just thinking about what he might do. I sure hope we don't see no little tombstones next to Mrs. Marlowe's no time soon."

Cass felt like someone punched him in the gut. "Thanks, Roscoe. Me too. Again, I want to thank all of you men for your help. I'll start my own search at daybreak in the morning."

Goose and Gander came running up to their father. "You want to watch us see-saw?"

He didn't, but he had made them a promise. Goat's letter came back to haunt him.

"Are you gonna watch us?"

"Sure. Let me see what you can do."

They crawled on separate ends of the board. Gander said, "Slide up a little, Goose, so you won't fall off."

The board hit the ground with a thud and Gander giggled while Goose's end was up in the air. She whimpered. "Stop it, Gander. Father, tell him to let me down."

Cass feigned a smile. "Well, I think you look like an angel, so high in the sky. But I need you two to run in the house, wash up and put on clean clothes. We're going on an adventure."

The excitement on their faces brought a real smile to his face.

"Where are we going?"

"Hurry and dress, and you'll see."

Even quicker than he'd imagined, the twins were outside, eager for an adventure and looking much better than when they went in.

The twins ordered a milkshake and a ham sandwich at Maude's, while Cass enjoyed a plate of liver and onions with mashed potatoes and a cup of strong coffee.

When they arrived back at the house, the twins ran and jumped on the see-saw, and Cass went to the shed to put the finishing touches on a sign he'd been working on. He put it in the car, then drove to the end of the road and placed it between the two columns. He stepped back and admired his work. "The Marlowe's Blest Nest."

He drove to the house and sent the twins inside to get ready for bed. After tucking them in, he walked down the stairs, and seeing Amelia reading in the Parlor, he went into the library, closing the door behind him. The temperature was dropping, and he built a fire in the fireplace, though the chill in the air outside the house couldn't match the frigid air on the inside.

His stomach knotted. It was evident Amelia intended to continue circulating that ridiculous story of a kidnapping. If he sat idly by, doing nothing to set the record straight, he'd be an accomplice to the lie. Yet, how could he tell the truth without having it get back to the twins that their mother put her own selfish desires ahead of them? He didn't know how he'd get her out of the house without upsetting the children, but she had to go.

The telephone rang. "Reverend Castle Marlowe, speaking."

"Reverend Marlowe, this is Dr. Biggs."

He felt as if his heart stopped. "My baby?"

"He's thriving. However, we need to keep him another week as a precaution, but your wife is being discharged. I'm sorry, I didn't realize you were leaving this morning, or you could've waited to take her with you."

He ran his hands through his hair. "It's okay. Please tell her I'll be there as soon as I can get there."

"No need to make a trip tonight. Just be here before eleven o'clock in the morning."

"I appreciate it, doctor, but I'm coming tonight."

Amelia said, "From what I heard, I'm guessing that was the doctor, saying Enoch is being discharged?"

He didn't answer but ran upstairs, left Gazelle a note in her room, and picked up the sleeping twins.

When he came down, Amelia groaned. "For goodness sake, Cass, you don't have to take them with you. I'm their mother. I can take care of them."

Cass felt Gander's arms tighten around his neck. "I want to go with Father."

****

Gazelle wandered around all afternoon, refusing to go home, though it began to appear she had no choice. She snapped her fingers when an idea popped in her head. Rebekah had an empty apartment. She'd go there and stay until her father and Rebekah returned from the hospital. She ran, hoping to get to the dress shop before Elsie locked up. Within a block, she saw Elsie standing outside, locking the door. Yelling, she said, "Elsie, please wait."

Elsie craned her neck and squinted in the semi-darkness. "Gazelle? Is that you?"

"Yes. I was hoping I could get here before you closed."

She smiled. "I'll be happy to open back up for you, sweetheart. I'll bet you're looking for a new bonnet to wear to the picnic, aren't you? You must have a special beau."

"Nothing like that. What I have to ask you is more important than the picnic."

"Does your father know you're out here this late?"

"Father's in Mobile at the hospital—"

"Oh, my. Is it your brother? I saw in the paper that he ran away. Did they find him? Is he hurt bad?"

"It's not Goat, and no they haven't found him, yet. It's my little brother, Gopher, but I've been walking for a long time. Can we please go in and sit down?"

"I have something better in mind. Suppose we walk over to Maude's and talk over supper. Have you had supper?"

"I haven't eaten anything all day."

"You poor dear."

Maude clomped over to their table with her hands planted on her hips. "The only thing left is liver and onions. Want it or not?"

Gazelle cringed. "I guess. If that's all you have."

"Why didn't you come with your Pa?"

Elsie rolled her eyes. "Excuse us, Maude. Could we please have a little privacy?"

"You can have all you want. I was just curious, that's all. Pardon me for buttin' in."

Though not particularly fond of liver, Gazelle ate every bite on her plate, before getting around to admitting why she was there.

Elsie sat silently, biting her lower lip. "Hon, let me see if I got this straight. Rebekah McAlister has been tending to you kids?"

"That's right. But Father called her, and she left immediately to see if her blood could be used to help Gopher."

"This doesn't make sense. Rebekah? My Rebekah? I can't believe she would've lied to me. Who can you trust, nowadays?" She rubbed her temples. "She left me a note, saying she was going to—" She paused, trying to recall exactly what was on the note. If I remember correctly, she said an emergency had come up and she wouldn't be able to come in for a few days, but she'd be back as soon as possible. And I haven't heard a word from her since."

Gazelle said, "But she didn't lie. I was with her when she wrote the note. Our housekeeper didn't show up that morning, and I came here to find you, because we needed help. Father was gone and Goose had the chicken pox. I saw a light on upstairs, and I thought you were there, but when I beat on the door, Rebekah came and unlocked it. I didn't know she lived here. I told her our situation, and she said she'd go help me."

The lines on Elsie's face relaxed. "I was wrong to be so hasty. Of course, she would do that. Rebekah's a very sensitive, compassionate young lady. Bless her heart, she's so young, herself, I'm sure she meant well, but I do wish she had stopped and told me, so I could've been the one to go. But what brought you here, tonight?"

"It's complicated, but I have a favor to ask."

"Anything, child."

"Since Rebekah isn't using the apartment, would you mind if I stayed there, tonight?"

"I wouldn't mind at all, but if your Father and Rebekah are

both in Mobile, I think I should take you back and stay with you and the children. I can put a 'Closed' sign on the door. I'll stay as long as you need me."

"You're very kind, but that isn't necessary. There's someone there with the kids. I just needed to get away for a while."

"Well, bless your heart, I'm sure this has been a very trying time for you. But I think you should call home and let them know where you are, so the housekeeper won't worry."

She nodded, reluctantly, holding crossed fingers behind her skirt.

When Maude showed signs of irritation, Elsie said, "I think she wants to close. Let's go back to the shop."

They walked back and Elsie unlocked the door. "I don't feel I should leave you in the apartment alone, so I'll stay with you."

"No, please. I'm not a baby. I'll soon be thirteen. Can't you trust me?"

"It's not a matter of trust. Aren't you afraid?"

"Of what?"

Elsie sighed. "I suppose it'll be fine, just for tonight. But in the morning, we need to get you back home. Don't forget to call the housekeeper, so she won't worry."

"Yes ma'am. I'm sorry to be a bother."

"No bother at all, child. I'm flattered that you came to me."

CHAPTER 31

Elsie waited for Gazelle to go upstairs, before leaving the dress shop. Her heart hammered as she locked the door behind her. This should prove to Cass that the children approved of her. Why else would Gazelle come looking for her? She knew in her heart the only reason Cass turned her away was because he feared she wouldn't make a good mother for his five children. Well, she'd show him. In the morning, she'd take Gazelle home and send the housekeeper on her way, and she'd have that household running like a fine made swiss clock before he returned. She'd dealt with all sorts of people for years, and after all, children were just little people. Besides, there were only three there, now. How hard could it be?

****

Gazelle tossed and turned all night. Her mind wouldn't shut down. If only she could find Goat. She went over the conversation again, when he claimed she wasn't listening. Well, she was listening now. She recalled him saying, "About five-hundred feet from the dock, there's a spot in the river where I've been catching a lot of crappy. I hardly ever throw a hook in there that I don't pull up a fish. Nobody knows about it but me. It's an eddy at the bend of the river, hidden by a clomp of reeds, so even when a boat passes, they don't see me." She popped her flat palm to her forehead. He'd also mentioned being in the bend when he heard her talking to Jeremiah. "That's it!"

At first light, she ran over to the livery stable and saw Mr. Josh Roland inside, feeding the horses. "Mr. Josh, I'm Preacher Marlowe's daughter, Gazelle, and I'm here to get our horse, Patches."

"Well, I'm sure he'll be happy to see you. Who was that young woman who left him here? "

"A friend of the family. I don't have any money, but—"

"Don't you fret yo' pretty little head. The preacher's good for it. Let me saddle 'er up for you."

"Thank you."

She hoped Elsie wouldn't be too upset with her for not waiting. By the time she reached the river, the sun was a little higher, making it easier to see where she was going as she rode Patches through the thick woods. She headed for the dock, saw the bend in the river and followed until she saw a clomp of reeds.

Thrashing her way through the bulrushes, cattails and tall reeds, she sniffed, then followed her nose and found Goat turning a rabbit on a firepit. He looked up and grinned. "I wondered why it was taking you so long."

"I just figured it out last night, or I would've been here sooner. Why didn't you bring me with you?"

He chuckled. "I thought I gave you pretty specific instructions." He pointed to the rabbit. "Ready for breakfast?"

She shook her head. "Not that hungry. I came to get you."

"Forget it, sissy. I'm not going back."

"You were wrong, Goat. Father didn't lie. When he told us Mother was dead, he thought she was."

"But he let us go on thinking she was dead, when he knew better."

"I think he was afraid she'd come and take us away from him."

"Why would she do that? She didn't want us, or she would never have left us."

"As leverage, to get him back. But Father has been sick with worry. He's had search parties looking for you since you left."

He grinned. "I know. I heard them wandering around. They came within feet of me and walked on by."

"Not only has he been worried about you—Gopher is in the hospital and may not live. But there's something else you don't know." She told him about their mother showing up at the house. "Please come back home, Goat. Not just for me, but Father doesn't need anything else to worry over."

"Did you say he's in Mobile, now?"

She nodded.

"Then why don't we catch a mess of fish before we go back. You *can* fry fish, can't you?"

She swatted him with her hand. "If you can clean them, I can fry them."

They fished for hours. Gazelle didn't know when she'd had so much fun, nor did she know when her irritating, annoying little brother grew up, but she liked what he'd become.

****

Elsie was shocked, when she opened the shop and discovered Gazelle wasn't there. Hoping she'd eventually show up with an explanation, Elsie stayed and worked 'til noon. But when there was still no sign of Gazelle, she put the 'Closed,' sign on the door and decided to go look for her. Maybe the housekeeper had insisted on the phone that she go home.

She slowed the car when she reached the arch. She grinned, seeing the new sign. "Well, it was about time! I got sick every time I passed by here."

Elsie knocked on the door and Goose came running down the hall. Opening the door, she let out a yell. "Mother, Elsie's here. Me and Gander are going to the creek to catch tadpoles."

Elsie's brow shot up. *Mother?* Surely, she misunderstood the child.

Amelia went to the door. "Elsie Drummond. What are you doing here?"

Elsie's eyes widened. "A better question would be, what are you doing here? I thought you were dead."

Amelia shrugged. "It's a long story, but suffice it to say, I was kidnapped and held against my will. Thank goodness, I'm home now to my wonderful children and my loving husband. Do you have a reason for paying a visit this morning?"

"I'm looking for Gazelle."

"And what business, may I ask, do you have with my daughter?"

"Funny you should ask. Didn't she tell you?"

Amelia wrung her hands and stumbled over her words. "Uh, I suppose she forgot to mention it before she went to bed, but, uh, I'm sure if she had considered it important, she would have said something."

"I'd like to speak with her."

"Sorry, She wasn't feeling well last night, so I'm letting her sleep late this morning."

"I have reason not to believe you."

"Get out of my house. You tried your best to get Cass when we were in high school, but he wanted me."

The front door opened, and Cass came walking in with Rebekah. Hearing the ruckus, he sat their bags in the hallway.

The two women stopped arguing and stood frozen in place. Then, Amelia walked over and wrapped her arm around Cass. "I'm glad you're home, darling. I miss you when you're gone. How's our little Gator?"

One corner of his lip curled. "Gator? He's Gopher, Amelia. And thanks to Rebekah, he's gonna live."

Rebekah said, "Elsie, what are you doing here?"

"I came looking for Gazelle. Amelia said she's upstairs, sleeping, but I happen to know she's lying, because Gazelle spent the night in your apartment last night. She was gone when I got there this morning. I think we should go looking for her."

Cass's mouth gaped open. "Where could she—" Before he could complete his sentence, Patches came galloping into the yard with two riders, Goat and Gazelle. He glanced out the window and yelled, "They're here. Both of them." He and Rebekah hurried out to meet them.

Goat held his head down, unable to look at his father. "I'm sorry for making you worry."

"Hey, the important thing is that you're back. This is a day to celebrate."

"But where's Gopher?"

"He's doing good, but the doctor wanted to keep him a few more days."

Goose and Gander came walking through the back door, and seeing Goat, they rushed him at the same time. Goose was crying. "You're back. We missed you. I thought you were dead."

He knelt down to hug them. "I'm very much alive, and I missed you, too."

Elsie said, "Well, I see my presence isn't needed here, but Rebekah, I'll expect you back at work tomorrow."

"About that, Elsie. I love making hats, but I'm afraid I'll be too busy in the future to be helping you at the shop."

Rebekah and Cass exchanged smiles. He pulled her close and said, "We have something to share with all of you."

Rebekah held out her left hand, revealing a wedding band.

Gazelle squealed. "Is it for real, this time?"

Cass nodded. "Just in case there was ever a question, the Chaplain at the hospital did a do-over before we left today."

Amelia's jaw flexed. "Cass, I'll fight it in court. I have the welfare of my children to consider. She's too young for you. Why, you foolish man, she's not much older than our daughter."

Cass edged up close to Amelia, then pulled out the letter. "If I were you, I'd get as far from this town as possible, because I have proof that you weren't kidnapped and I won't hesitate to have it printed in the paper if you stick around. As far as the people in this town know, you drowned. You may wish you had, if the truth gets out."

"Don't threaten me, Cass. You wouldn't dare, for the children's sake."

"It's for the sake of the children, I will definitely do it. Leave town, Amelia. There's not room here for both of us."

Elsie laughed at Amelia's little hissy fit, then threw her arms around Rebekah. "Well, I think it's wonderful. Cass, you're a very lucky man. You couldn't have found a better bride. Frankly, I wish it could've been me, but I'm just very glad it's not *her*," she said, gesturing toward Amelia.

Goose pulled on Rebekah's skirt. "Can I be the flower girl at the wedding?"

Gazelle said, "Goose, there won't be a wedding. Father and Rebekah are—"

Rebekah blurted, "Oh, but there *will* be a wedding, and yes, you can, sweetheart!" She knelt down and holding Goose's hands, said, "You'll make a lovely flower girl. And Gazelle will be the bride's maid, Gander will be the ring bearer, and Goat will be his father's best man. The wedding will be in the parlor at six o'clock this evening. Can everyone be ready?"

Goose jumped up and down squealing. "I can, but I need lots of flowers to drop on the floor. That's what a flower girl does. But what about Miss Elsie? What can she do?"

Elsie laughed. "I'll be the one to give Rebekah away."

Goose grabbed Rebekah around her legs and squeezed. "This is gonna be the happiest day of my life. I've never been a flower girl."

They heard the door slam, looked out and saw dust flying as Amelia drove out of the yard.

Elsie said, "All new brides deserve a honeymoon. Have you thought about where you'd like to go?"

Rebekah looked at Cass and nodded. "We'd both love to be at the hospital with our little Gopher, but I'm afraid that won't be possible."

"Nonsense. If that's where you choose to be, then plan on it. I'll bring my sewing machine here, and maybe I could teach Gazelle to make hats while you're gone."

Gazelle shrieked. "You mean it? I'd love that."

"Then it's settled." She hugged the newlyweds, then added, "All's well that ends well, and this day is certainly ending well." She reached for her purse and Rebekah said, "You can't leave yet. The wedding is in a few hours."

"I won't be gone long."

Cass and Rebekah didn't see much of the children for the remainder of the afternoon, since the kids were upstairs rehearsing their parts.

He put his arm around his wife and pulled her close. "I have a little errand to run. It won't take long."

"Just make sure you're back by six o'clock."

He chuckled. "Trust me, I wouldn't miss it."

Elsie hurried back to her house. She ran upstairs, opened her hope chest and pulled out the beautiful white wedding dress, covered with fine lace and hundreds of tiny seed pearls. She threaded the machine and took in a couple of darts on either side, then held it up and smiled. "It should fit perfectly. This dress was meant to be worn at Cass's wedding." She found the veil and satin shoes and hurried back to help Rebekah get ready for a wedding.

Cass drove to the Flower Shop and ordered every rose in stock. The florist went through them all, through several in the trash, explaining they were wilting and would soon be losing their petals.

"I'll take them. I have a beautiful little flower girl that will love tossing the petals on the floor." He made one more stop before going back to the house. It was all set.

Elsie ran out to meet him. "Don't go in the Guest Room. You can't see the bride before the wedding."

"Then do something with these." He handed her the flowers.

"I know exactly what to do. But I need lots of Magnolia leaves."

Cass brought back an armful of branches and within thirty minutes, Elsie had the Parlor looking like a beautiful wedding chapel, with the arch over the door covered with white satin ribbons and large, lovely magnolia leaves. She decorated the mantle and windows with roses, while holding out several stems for a bride's bouquet, three boutonnieres, and filled a basket with rose petals.

At five 'til six, Sam and Lolita came riding up on Cass's old buggy. Cass let them in and directed Lolita to the piano.

Gazelle, enjoying her role as wedding coordinator, led the children down the stairs, eager for the ceremony to go off without a hitch.

Cass stood in front of the fireplace beside Sam.

The Guest room door opened, and Lolita began to play, "Here Comes the Bride."

Cass's jaw dropped and the children oohed and ahhed when they saw the beautiful bride.

Gander held a pillow with a ring on top, and Goose came walking down the hall and into the parlor, dropping delicate red rose petals along the way.

One would've thought Sam was a real preacher, the way he performed the ceremony. As soon as he said, "The groom may now kiss the bride," Cass saw Goat rush out the door, then breathed a sigh of relief when he came back in, holding his father's suitcase in one hand and Rebekah's carpetbag in the other.

Goat looked at his father and winked. "I saw you drop your bags in the hallway when you came in. I'll go put them where they belong."

Rebekah felt a blush paint her face when he headed straight for Cass's bedroom. Her husband's hand reached for hers and gave a little squeeze.

"Welcome home, Mrs. Marlowe."

CHALKBOARD PREACHER

I've won numerous literary awards throughout the years, but the awesome friends I've met on this journey have been my true reward. Below is a listing of my novels:

SWITCHED SERIES:

*Lunacy – Book 1
*Unwed – Book 2
*Mercy – Book 3

GRAVE ENCOUNTER SERIES

*When the Tide Ebbs – Book 1
*When the Tide Rushes In – Book 2
*When the Tide Turns – Book 3

THE KEEPER SERIES

*The Keeper – Book 1
*The Prey – Book 2
*The Destined – Book 3

HOMECOMING SERIES:

*Sweet Lavender – A Novel -Book 1
*Unforgettable – A novella - 2
*Gonna Sit Right Down – A novella- 3
*Hello Walls – A novella - 4

PLOW HAND – Stand-alone
A GIRL CALLED ALABAMA – *Stand-alone*
CHALKBOARD PREACHER FROM VINEGAR BEND – *Book 1 of Vinegar Bend Series*

Thank you for choosing my books. An Amazon review would be greatly appreciated. I love hearing from my readers! Email me at,

Kay@kaychandler.info

Made in the USA
Columbia, SC
31 August 2020